"Hugo," she conceded, taking another deep breath to calm herself down. "I'm here on a professional basis."

"So you are. Sorry for confusing the issue." His smile was very white and patently apologetic, so why was she thinking of a wolf in sheep's clothing?

It was the animal thing again. Male on the prowl.

All her instincts were picking it up and reacting to it, throwing her into a fluster because he was terribly attractive and the situation was making her feel more vulnerable than she should be.

"Though I can't help thinking how fortuitous this meeting is," he ran on. "Both of us... currently unattached..."

Had he read her mind? Those blue eyes were dynamite.

"...and I do, indeed, like what I see."

It was a very pointed statement of personal interest and intent. He wanted her. Or at least wanted to try her out, see how she fitted with him.

MISTRESS
TO A
MILLIONAIRE

She's his in the bedroom,
but he can't buy her love....

The ultimate fantasy becomes a reality.

Live the dream with more
MISTRESS TO A MILLIONAIRE titles
by some of your much-loved
Harlequin Presents® authors.

Emma Darcy

HIS BOUGHT MISTRESS

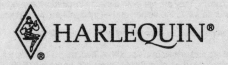

TORONTO • NEW YORK • LONDON
AMSTERDAM • PARIS • SYDNEY • HAMBURG
STOCKHOLM • ATHENS • TOKYO • MILAN • MADRID
PRAGUE • WARSAW • BUDAPEST • AUCKLAND

ISBN 0-373-12439-2

HIS BOUGHT MISTRESS

First North American Publication 2005.

Copyright © 2004 by Emma Darcy.

www.eHarlequin.com

Printed in U.S.A.

CHAPTER ONE

ANGIE BLESSING did not feel particularly blessed on this fine summer Sunday morning. In fact, the bright sunshine was giving her a headache. Or maybe it was her relationship with Paul that was giving her the headache.

Here she was, sitting in his Mercedes convertible, being driven home to the apartment she shared with her best friend and business partner, Francine Morgan—her choice because she didn't want to go yacht-racing with Paul today—and instead of thinking how lucky she was to be the love interest in the life of one of Sydney's most eligible bachelors, she was thinking of Francine's current bible: *The Marriage Market After Thirty—Finding the Right Husband For You.*

For the past three years she'd been Paul Overton's *partner.*

No proposal of marriage.

The really troubling part was, if he got down on his knees right now and asked her to marry him, Angie wasn't sure she'd say yes.

'Don't forget we've got the fund-raising dinner next Friday night,' he tossed at her as he drove down her road at Cremorne, conveniently situated on his way to the Royal North Shore Yacht Club.

More politics, Angie thought. Just like the party last night. Everything with Paul was politics, making influential connections, building a network of pow-

erful support that would back his ambition to go into
parliament. His current career as a barrister had little
to do with a love of the law. It was more a showcase
for his rhetorical skills, a step towards what he really
wanted.

'Angie…?' He threw a frown at her, impatient with
her silence.

'Yes, Paul. It's marked in my calendar,' she said
dutifully, hating the way she was little more than an
ornament on his arm at such functions. 'And we have
the ballet on Wednesday night,' she reminded him,
relieved at being able to look forward to that date.

'I don't think I'll be able to go. The case I'm on
this week needs a lot of preparation. Big trial, as you
know, and the media will be covering it.'

Angie gritted her teeth. Ballet was *her* thing. But,
of course, that wasn't important to his career. He
could have worked on his case preparation today instead of yacht-racing, though naturally it wouldn't occur to Paul to give up one of his pleasures.

'Take Francine with you,' he suggested brightly.

'Right!' she bit out. No point in arguing. Waste of
breath.

He pulled the Mercedes into the kerb outside her
apartment block, engine idling, which meant he
wasn't about to get out and open the passenger door
for her. Angie wondered if the romance went out of
every relationship after three years. Was being taken
for granted the norm?

Paul beamed her a rueful smile. 'Hope the queasy
stomach settles down soon.'

Her excuse for not spending today with him.

She returned the smile. 'Me, too.'

He wasn't going to kiss her. Couldn't afford to catch a tummy bug with the big trial on this week.

'You do look peaky,' he commented sympathetically. 'Look after yourself, Angie.'

He wasn't about to, she thought.

'I'll call you during the week,' he added.

Sure. To check I'm okay for Friday night when you need me again.

'Fine,' she said, struggling to rise above her jaundiced mind-set.

Paul was the most handsome man she'd ever met: tall, broad-shouldered, instantly impressive, dark wavy hair swept back from what she thought of as a noble forehead, riveting dark eyes that captivated with their sharp intelligence, a strong male face to complement his very male physique. He came from a wealthy family, was wealthy himself, and she could share a brilliant future with him if he ever got around to offering it.

'Have a nice day,' she forced out, then opened the door and swung herself out of the car.

She watched him drive off—the A-list man in his A-list car—and seriously wondered if Paul saw her as an A-list woman. She probably projected the right image: tall, long blond hair, slim enough to wear any clothes well, though her figure was too curvy for classic model proportions, good skin that didn't need make-up to cover blemishes, the kind of clear-boned face that always photographed well though she certainly didn't consider herself beautiful. Her eyes were her most attractive feature, probably because they were an unusual sage green.

When it came to self-presentation, she was good, having learnt that this art was an asset in her line of business. People who hired professional help from an interior design company had more confidence in a professional who was well groomed and colour co-ordinated herself. She definitely had the image Paul liked but did she have the right *substance* for him to consider her marriageable?

Was being a successful career woman enough?

No wealthy family in her background. No political pull there, either. Her parents were both artists with antigovernment attitudes, perfectly happy for their daughter to make her own choices in life, but staunchly into alternative society themselves. They were hardly the right people for Paul to have as in-laws, though Angie knew her parents would never thrust themselves into *his* limelight.

Besides, they lived so far away, right up the north coast at Byron Bay. They'd never actually been a factor in her relationship with Paul, not like *his* parents who seemed to accept her. On the surface. But was she suitable as a lifetime partner? More importantly, did she want to be Paul Overton's lifetime partner?

It had once been a dazzling prospect.

Now, Angie wasn't so sure.

In fact, she was beginning to feel she might well have wasted three years on a rosy dream which was fast developing wilting edges. She headed into the apartment block, wondering if Francine had found her Mr. Right last night at the *Dinner for Six*—a group of thirty-something singles wanting to meet their match, this being her friend's latest dating ploy in hunting for a husband.

She found Francine sitting on their balcony over-looking the bay, Sunday newspapers spread on the table in front of her, a mug of coffee to hand, and the gloom of failure denying any interest in the lovely morning or anything else. She was still in her pyjamas. Her dark curly hair was an unbrushed tangle. Smudges of last night's mascara gave her grey eyes a bruised look. Slumped shoulders added to her air of dejection.

'Struck out again?' Angie asked sympathetically, stepping outside to join her friend.

'Too earnest. No spark,' came the listless reply.

The thirty-something men were probably as desperate to impress as Francine was, Angie thought. 'Maybe they'd be more relaxed on a second date.'

'Bor...ing.' Francine rolled her eyes at her. 'And they'd be all over me like a flash if I gave them a second chance. Hot to trot, all of them.'

'Well, you did look hot in that red dress last night.'

Positively stunning, Angie had thought, the fabric clinging to Francine's gym-toned body, plus some provocative cleavage showing due to the purchase of a new push-up bra. Her figure was petite but certainly very feminine. Pretty face. Gorgeous hair. Francine was a knockout when she set out to be aggressively attractive.

'I need to light a fire in the right guy when I meet him,' she expounded. 'That's what the book says. Stand out from the crowd. Be positive and memorable. Always look my best.'

'Not exactly practising that this morning,' Angie teased, trying to lighten her up. 'What if I'd walked in here with a friend of Paul's in tow?'

'So I would have blown it. I'm just having some down time. Besides, you're not supposed to be here. What happened to yacht-racing?'

She shrugged. 'I didn't feel like it.'

'Easy for some,' Francine muttered darkly, then slammed her hands on the table and rose to her feet. 'Okay. Clean myself up. Go to the gym. Spread myself around. I'm doing it.' Grim resolve was in her voice and on her face as she marched off towards the bathroom.

'You might need to relax more yourself.' The words tripped out before Angie could think better of them.

Francine wheeled on her, spitting mad. 'Don't give me advice! You've had your Mr. Right for so long you don't know how it is for me, Angie. Or what it's like out there on the dating scene. And I'm not settling for just anyone!'

'Neither you should,' Angie quickly agreed, not even sure that *settling* for Paul was an option. Her confidence in his rightness for her was also at an all-time low.

'All these years, building up our business, you said yourself I'm brilliant at marketing our design company,' Francine ran on heatedly.

'You are,' Angie acknowledged.

'I've even snagged the Fullbright contract for us.'

A plum contract, worth a lot of money to them.

'So I should be able to market myself and get the result I want,' Francine said decisively. 'That means I have to sell what my husband-to-be finds appealing. And let me tell you I'm not going to leave any stone unturned. I'm thirty years old and I want a husband and children in my future.'

Having delivered this firm declaration, Francine marched on to the bathroom.

They were *both* thirty years old, Angie thought, taking her friend's empty mug to the kitchen, intent on brewing some fresh coffee for herself. They'd spent their twenties establishing their business, working hard, climbing up in the world. The Fullbright contract proved they'd reached the top level in their field—being given the job of colour co-ordinating a fabulous new block of luxury apartments situated right on the harbour shoreline. That success should be very sweet. And it was. But they were women, too, and priorities definitely changed as the biological clock started ticking.

Angie told herself she probably shouldn't be feeling so discontented with Paul. So what if the excitement and passion in their first year together had waned! It probably did in every relationship, giving way to a comfortable sense of being able to count on each other. It was unrealistic to expect everything to be perfect. Hadn't she accepted that maintaining something workable demanded a fair amount of compromise?

Except Paul never compromised on anything.

She hadn't noticed this at first. Now she was probably noticing it too much. But if she broke off with him…It was scary to think of herself being suddenly single again, out there in the thirty-something dating scene. Francine's total dedication to her mission seemed far too extreme to her, yet…would she begin to feel just as desperate, given no readily available prospects?

Maybe she should count her blessings with Paul instead of being critical.

Yet he had never once brought up the subject of marriage.

Three years…

Was he ever going to?

Was she just a handy habit to him, one he'd shed when the time came to make a marriage that suited his ambitions?

The coffee percolater pinged, and she poured herself a mugful, then wandered back out to the balcony with it, her mind hopelessly riddled with doubts.

The newspapers did not provide the soothing distraction she needed. Angie tried focusing her thoughts on the Fullbright contract, planning how best to handle the scheduled meeting with Hugo Fullbright himself, scheduled for next Thursday morning. The billionaire property developer was bound to be demanding and she'd need to impress him with her answers. At least she was confident of achieving that.

Francine re-emerged, looking very bright and bouncy, dressed in spectacular lime green lycra shorts and a matching midriff top, ready for her trip to the gym. 'I've made up my mind,' she announced. 'I'm going to spread my net wider.'

'A new strategy?' Angie queried.

'I've spent eight months doing what the book recommends with only dud results. The thing to do now is grab attention big-time.'

'How?'

'I read about a really bold scheme in the newspaper. I get my photo scanned, blown up, and plastered on a billboard placed at a busy city intersection. Anyone interested can contact me on the Internet.'

Angie's jaw dropped in shock. 'A billboard!' she gasped.

'Major public exposure,' Francine rattled on, apparently uncaring about any negative outcomes. 'Should bring in a huge number of guys for me to choose from.'

'You're using your face and name on a public billboard?' Angie was appalled. 'What about crackpots and perverts and...'

'Not my *real* name. More of a teaser which will be a password to reach me through a third party on the Net. I'll be protected, Angie.'

'But people will recognise your face.'

'So? No harm in being a celebrity. Probably do me a power of good.'

'Francine, what about our business associates? What are they going to think?'

'I don't care what they think. Business is business. We deliver what our clients want. Nothing wrong with me going after what *I* want.'

'But a billboard...it's so...so public!'

'Are you going to be ashamed of me?' Francine bored in belligerently.

'No! No, of course not. I'm just worried for you. What you might end up having to handle.'

'Let me worry about that. I'm simply giving you fair warning so you don't get a shock when the billboard goes up. I'm off to the gym now.'

Cutting off any further argument.

Angie didn't like the idea one bit. It horrified her. On the other hand, she wasn't a go-getter type, not like Francine whose job it was to bring in the interior design contracts for Angie to work on. In any event, nothing she said was going to change her friend's mind, and it was probably better to stay silent on the highly sensitive issue of how to reel in Mr. Right.

Angie hoped Paul wouldn't see the billboard.

He'd be scathing about her friend's blatant self-publicity.

But it wasn't *his* life and he would never have

Francine's problems. Any amount of eager women would leap at the chance to be Paul Overton's Miss Right, no need for him to advertise what a prize he was. Angie decided she would stick loyally by Francine, regardless of the consequences of her scheme.

Three days later, the inevitable was announced. 'It will be up tomorrow,' Francine informed her as they settled in their seats at the ballet. Her eyes were dancing with excited anticipation.

'Up where?' Angie asked, trying her utmost to hold back any dampener on the happy sparkles.

'You'll see it on your way to the Fullbright meeting tomorrow.'

And see it she did the next morning.

No one crossing the Sydney Harbour Bridge by car, bus, train or foot could miss it. Angie almost drove into the back of the car in front of her. Not because she was agog at seeing Francine's face on the billboard. She'd been mentally prepared to see it somewhere.

The shock—and it was totally mind-blasting—was in seeing her own face on the billboard.

Hers!

And underneath it the caption—*Foxy Angel*!

CHAPTER TWO

HUGO FULLBRIGHT had a very good view of the billboard as the cars in front of his slowed to a crawl approaching the toll booths at the southern end of the bridge. It amused him to check out the passing parade of people brave enough to hang themselves out in public. Six new faces on it this morning. The blonde stirred his interest. *Foxy Angel.*

Few women looked that good. Probably a computer enhanced photograph. Undoubtedly she would prove a disappointment to the guys who leapt on her bandwagon. Logic insisted that something had to be wrong for *her* to need this medium to get a man. But she sure was a winner on the billboard.

Foxy Angel... Hugo grinned over the teaser. Great marketing. Intriguing suggestion of naughty but nice. Just the mix he liked himself. Except he didn't care for the *naughty* part to be inspired and driven by cocaine.

It had hit him like a brick when he'd found Chrissie snorting a line of it at the party last Saturday night. And her argument—'But, darling, sex is so much more fun when I'm on a high.'—was not what a man wanted to hear, as though the pleasure he gave didn't do enough for her.

Goodbye, Chrissie.

Hugo had no regrets over that decision. To his mind, people who depended on recreational drugs to *perform* weren't in control of themselves or anything

15

else. He didn't tolerate it in any of the top executives
in his company and he wasn't about to tolerate it in
the woman closest to him. Besides, illegal substances
were illegal, bound to lead to messy situations.

Having passed over the bridge and beyond sight of
the tantalising photo on the billboard, Hugo concentrated his mind on the fast approaching meeting with
the colour co-ordinator for his new Pyrmont development. He'd purchased three old warehouses along
the harbour front, then had them torn down to accommodate this project. Since he'd be putting million-
dollar prices on each luxury apartment, he wanted a
top class job done on their visual presentation.

It was important to impress that on the specialist
he'd contracted, so best he did it personally, let the
woman know he wasn't interested in any cost-cutting
that might have a negative effect. A quality finish was
essential. He was happy with the architectural design
but *the finish* should be the icing on the cake.

Attention to detail—that was the key to success.

Nothing overlooked.

One of the ground floor apartments had been turned
into a temporary business centre for on the job requirements and supervision. Hugo mentally approved
the security system for the garage as he parked his
car, and the exclusive access system to each apartment as he moved on to enter the company *office*. He
greeted his people there, left instructions for Miss
Blessing to be escorted to the meeting room, and for
refreshments to be brought ten minutes after she arrived.

The meeting room had been set up at the far end
of the open living area where a wall of glass allowed
a spectacular view of the harbour and its ever-

changing traffic. It comprised a rented lounge setting with a large square coffee table. Hugo didn't bother sitting down. He stood looking out, watching various boats going past—cruisers, yachts, ferries—glancing at his watch to check the time.

The woman was late. Five minutes. Ten minutes. Unpunctuality always niggled him. It disregarded the value of his time, invariably shortening his temper. When he finally heard the footsteps signalling her arrival, he had to school himself not to display impatience as he swung around to greet her.

In actual fact, any sense of impatience shot right out of his mind as recognition hit. The long blond hair was swinging naturally around her shoulders just as he'd imagined it could, the face was an exact replica, no computerised touch-up to make her features more attractive, no blemishes on that glowing skin, and the unusual green eyes were even more fascinating in real life...

Foxy Angel!

Not only living up to her photograph, but delivering the complete goods with stunning oomph!

Her figure was femme fatale class—lush curves where there should be lush curves, stunningly outlined by a citrine silk dress that shouted sensuality, and long shapely legs enhanced by sexy strappy high-heels. High impact stuff. No doubt about it. Hugo felt a hot tingling in his groin, a charge of adrenalin shooting through his body, excitement fizzing in his brain.

It was fantastic luck that Chrissie was gone from his life, because this woman was walking into it, ringing bells that said he had to have her.

And she was available!

The trick was to win her before a horde of eager beavers jumped on the billboard bandwagon.

Angie was used to guys giving her the once-over but Hugo Fullbright's comprehensive head to foot appraisal felt more sexual than most and it bothered her. It bothered her even more that he made no attempt to switch to business meeting mode. And he looked unbelievably sexy himself, stunning blue eyes simmering with bedroom interest, a tantalising little smile that smacked of sensual satisfaction lurking on his mouth as he watched her walk towards him.

A wave of his hand dismissed her escort.

His focus did not deviate from Angie, and her heart gave an agitated skip as she realised Hugo Fullbright was probably a blitz operator in more than property development. Paul might be classical male but this guy was animal male in spades. And he radiated the kind of magnetic intensity Russell Crowe brought to his movies.

His thick black hair was cut short but it still had an untamed look about it. His skin was darkly tanned, suggesting he lived more under the sun than away from it. His body was encased in tailored sophistication—a beautiful grey suit that had a sheen of blue silk running through it—yet she had the sense of a strong, lithe physique, like that of a big jungle cat, wired to pounce.

It took all her willpower to step up to him, offer her hand, and make her vocal chords perform at a natural pitch. 'Mr. Fullbright, I'm Angie Blessing.'

'Angie...' He rolled her name off his tongue as though tasting it for honey. The vivid blue eyes twinkled with wicked teasing. 'Short for Angel?'

Her heart sank like a stone. He'd seen the billboard, connected her to it. 'No. Angela,' she answered sharply, desperate for some diversion. 'But everyone calls me Angie.'

'I think Angel suits you better,' he mused, holding on to her hand, his thumb fanning her skin, shooting heat into her bloodstream.

She felt her cheeks burning. Her mind was torn over what to do—ignore the allusion to the billboard or confront it? This was business. Business! It was wrong to get into anything personal.

'I do apologise for being late, Mr. Fullbright,' she rushed out.

'Hugo.' He smiled invitingly.

'I had an urgent call…'

'I imagine you'll be getting many urgent calls. I'm sure I'm not the only man who…*likes what he sees.*'

The direct reference to the words on the billboard—*If you like what you see, contact…*—was too pointed for Angie to dismiss. She took a deep breath and plunged straight into trying to clear the murky waters of this meeting.

'Mr. Fullbright…'

'Hugo,' he slid in, and started to lift her hand as though he intended to kiss it!

She snatched it out of his grasp, firmly claiming, 'A mistake was made!'

He moved his now empty hand into a lazily elegant gesture that requested more information. 'A mistake?'

'The person who composed that billboard used the wrong half of a photograph sent in by my friend,' she said heatedly, Francine's frantic excuse doing little to stop her blood from boiling on this issue.

'A friend,' Hugo Fullbright repeated mockingly,

not believing a word of it. Then he grinned. 'You don't have to hide behind a friend, Angie. I'm not in the least perturbed by your enterprising move. It cuts straight to the chase, doing away with any need for preliminary manoeuvres. I admire the sheer nerve of it.'

Angie realised that nothing she said was going to change his mind. The *friend* cover was too often used to insert distance from a personal interest. He'd seen her image on the billboard and any mistake seemed too improbable. Angie wondered if she could sue the billboard people for damages. Francine had promised to fix everything but Francine wasn't here right now and somehow Angie had to get this meeting on a business footing. It didn't matter what he *thought,* as long as he...

'I'm just letting you know you needn't be *foxy* about this,' he dropped into the silence, benevolently forgiving what he saw as pretence. 'In fact...'

'Mr. Fullbright,' she swiftly cut in.

'Please make it Hugo.' Charm on full blast, making her heart pitter-pat like a fluttering shuttlecock being batted around her chest.

'Hugo,' she conceded, taking another deep breath to calm herself down. 'I'm here on a professional basis.'

'So you are. Sorry for confusing the issue.' His smile was very white and patently apologetic, so why was she thinking of a wolf in sheep's clothing?

It was the animal thing again.

Male on the prowl.

All her instincts were picking it up and reacting to it, throwing her into a fluster because he was terribly attractive and the situation was making her feel more vulnerable than she should be. She'd been with Paul for three years and this man...she couldn't imagine this man without a woman in tow, married or otherwise.

'Though I can't help thinking how fortuitous this meeting is,' he ran on. 'Both of us...currently unattached...'

Had he read her mind? Those blue eyes were dynamite.

'...and I do, indeed, like what I see.'

It was a very pointed statement of personal interest and intent. He wanted her. Or, at least, wanted to try her out, see how she fitted with him.

And to Angie's intense embarrassment, she felt her body responding positively to it, telling her in no uncertain terms that she would like to have the experience of this man on a very personal level.

In spite of her attachment to Paul!

'Could we...' She swallowed hard to remove the weird constriction in her throat. 'Could we talk business now?' Her voice sounded slurred, husky, desperate, embarrassing her further.

A delaying tactic. A *foxy* tactic. His interpretation of this request danced through the amusement in his eyes. 'By all means tell me...what you want to tell me,' he invited, gesturing to the lounge setting. 'Would you like to sit down?'

'Yes. Thank you,' she jerked out, and hoped her suddenly tremulous legs would carry her to the leather sofa without any graceless teetering in her high-heeled sandals.

She made the move without mishap, deliberately choosing to seat herself in the centre of the sofa, delivering the hint for him to settle for an armchair, leaving her with enough personal space to feel comfortable. Which he did. Though it didn't lessen her physical awareness of him one bit. In fact, it was probably heightened, being able to see all of him, sitting with a relaxed waiting air, confident he would eventually get the outcome he wanted one way or another.

Angie fiercely concentrated on business, determined to stay professional. 'I don't know how hands-on you are on this project...' she started.

Disastrously.

Because he instantly inserted, 'My involvement in any project is never without a hands-on approach.' The quirky little smile had a double-edged kick as he added, 'You have my full attention, Angie.'

'Right!' She wished he wouldn't keep sucking the breath out of her. 'The concept I've decided upon for designing the colour co-ordination in these apartments...'

'I've already approved the concept.'

Oh great! Now he was pulling the mat out from under her professional feet. 'Then why am I here? What point is there to this meeting?' she demanded, losing her cool under the barrage of heat she felt coming from him.

His straight black eyebrows slanted in a kind of quizzical self-examination of his motives. 'Well, I'd have to say it's developed more points since I made the initial request.'

Since he saw her photo, advertising she was available!

Angie gritted her teeth, waiting for a *business* answer.

He grinned, aiming all his megawatt masculinity at

her. 'But the primary aim was simply to meet you and assess for myself if you will deliver what you promise.'

Her stomach curled. The only assessment going on in his eyes was centred on how much pleasure he might find in having her with him on a very personal level—whether she'd live up to whatever he thought she'd been advertising on the billboard!

'We have a contract,' she bit out. 'Ask anyone our company has dealt with. We have always honoured our contracts and delivered on schedule.'

'That has been checked, Angie,' he smoothly assured her. 'But even within the letter of the contract, some things can be fiddled and often are.'

Foxy.

Was that word going to haunt her on this job?

'What I want is a quality finish,' he continued. 'No cost cutting.'

'The prices we've quoted on materials are precise,' she shot in, emphatically adding, 'We have never compromised on quality. It wouldn't even occur to us to do so in this job. Our design company has a reputation to maintain.'

'And I willingly concede you do project a high-quality image, Angie.' Warm appreciation in his eyes. Too warm. 'It reinforces my feeling that I've made the right choice.'

His choice.

As though she had no say in it!

On the other hand, if he was talking about giving them the contract...best not to make any reply. Besides, her chest had tightened up again, rendering her breathless and speechless.

Hugo Fullbright smiled his white wolf smile. 'I just

wanted to impress on you that I don't believe in cutting costs when going after what I want.'

'Fine!' she choked out.

'So we now have an understanding of where we both stand,' he concluded.

'Yes.'

Point achieved, meeting over. Angie told herself to get up and take her leave. She uncrossed her ankles, planted her feet on the floor, ready to rise from the sofa...

'I'm flying to Tokyo tomorrow morning,' he tossed at her. 'Back Sunday night. What you might call a long weekend.'

Angie remained poised where she was, wondering what this had to do with her.

'A bit of business,' he explained offhandedly. 'I built a resort in Queensland for a Japanese consortium. They probably want to run other plans past me but primarily it's a hospitality trip—wining, dining, sightseeing.'

'Nice for you,' she commented, not knowing how else to respond.

'For you, too, Angie...' A wicked challenge sparkled in his eyes. '...if you'd like to come with me.'

Tokyo.

She'd never been to Japan.

And being whisked off there by him...

Shocked at these wayward thoughts—he was *wickedly* attractive—Angie pulled herself together and frantically tried to find an appropriate reply. Rejection in this situation was very tricky.

'Thank you. But I've never thought it a good idea to mix business with pleasure. It could develop into an awkward situation between us.'

'I would agree…if you worked directly for me. But you'll be working independently on this contract. Your own boss with absolute autonomy.' The white wolf smile flashed again. 'In fact, this trip may very well provide some beneficial business contacts for you and your design company.'

He was so smooth.

And appealing.

Even making business mixed with pleasure a plus instead of a minus.

Angie couldn't believe how tempted she was. Accepting such a proposition was tantamount to being gobbled up by this marauding man. It would be such a wild thing to do. Besides, there was Paul. The fundraiser dinner on Friday night. Why hadn't she thought of that before?

'I'm sorry. I have other plans—commitments—this weekend.'

'Fair enough,' he accepted gracefully, though his eyes were weighing how serious her commitments might be.

Angie flushed with embarrassment as she remembered the billboard—the vast flood of replies Francine was expecting through the Internet. Was Hugo thinking she wanted to check them out before picking *him?*

Useless to state again that her photo was a mistake.

No way would he buy the friend excuse.

She pushed up from the sofa, too agitated to remain seated a moment longer. 'Thank you for your time. I hope you have a great trip to Tokyo,' she rattled out, forcing the offer of her hand to make a polite, *businesslike* farewell.

He stood up in all his overpowering maleness, making Angie quake inside. Instead of taking her hand, he reached inside his suit jacket and extracted a slim, gold card-holder. 'Let me give you my card.' He opened it and pressed all his contact details into her hand, smiling a sensual promise as he said, 'Should you change your mind about Tokyo...give me a call.'

'Yes. Thank you,' she babbled, and somehow managed to stretch her mouth into a bright smile. 'Goodbye.'

'Until next time,' he purred.

Jungle cat, just biding his time for another opportunity to pounce.

Angie could feel him watching her walk away from him. Every nerve in her body was tingling as though a field of highly charged electricity was emanating from him. His card was burning in her hand. She tried to think of Paul—Paul who might or might not marry her—but Hugo Fullbright and a trip to Tokyo with him were terrible distractions.

Of course she couldn't do it.

She wouldn't.

She wasn't the type of person to throw all caution to the winds, dump a man who had every reason to expect love and loyalty from her, and leap into a relationship with someone else.

It just wasn't right.

CHAPTER THREE

THE moment Angie stepped into their official office and showroom at the trendy end of Glebe Road, Francine leapt to her feet from behind her desk and was in full spout, frantically trying to appease the wrath she felt coming her way, the forerunner of it being the urgent call that had made Angie late for her meeting with Hugo Fullbright.

'I've been onto the billboard people. Told them you were threatening to sue for damages. They apologised profusely for the mistake, but they can't get your photo off and mine on until tomorrow. They'll print a public apology if you want, Angie. I know it's partly my fault for giving them the photo of the two of us, but it was the best one ever taken of me, and I swear it was clearly specified which half to use. I don't know why the technician got it wrong. But I'm terribly, terribly sorry that he did.'

Her wildly flapping hands moved into wringing. 'Did…ummh…Hugo Fullbright recognise you like you thought he might?' Her grimace imagined the worst but anxiously hoped for a let off.

Angie heaved a long loosening-up sigh, resigning herself to the fact that what was done was done. A mistake had been made and Francine had clearly worked hard at correcting the situation, so there was no point in carrying on about it.

'Yes, he did recognise me,' she answered, rolling her eyes to lighten the fraught mood. 'He had *Foxy*

Angel on his mind from the moment I walked into the meeting.' Which reminded her to ask, 'Why on earth did you pick that name? He related it straight to Angie.'

Francine scrunched up her shoulders as though defending herself from an imminent attack. 'I thought it would appeal to men's fantasies.'

'Well, it certainly did the trick,' Angie dryly informed her, though everything Hugo Fullbright had aimed at her had not felt like a fantasy at all. It had been very direct and highly disturbing.

'Were you…horribly embarrassed?'

'Yes, I was horribly embarrassed.' *And tempted.* Though best to put that out of her mind now. 'Hugo Fullbright didn't believe the billboard photo was a mistake. He said he admired my nerve and invited me to accompany him to Tokyo for a dirty weekend.'

If she put it in those terms, the temptation would go away. It was probably true, too, if he thought the billboard photo meant she'd do anything for a man.

Francine's jaw dropped.

Angie had to smile.

Tit for tat in the shock department.

'A pity it wasn't you at the meeting,' Angie ran on, needing to lighten up about what had happened. 'Hugo Fullbright is as handsome as the devil, as wealthy as they come, plus sex appeal in spades and currently unattached. You missed out on quite a catch!'

'Damn!' Shock collapsed into disappointment at the lost opportunity. 'All my meetings leading up to signing the contract were with the architect and he was seriously married with children. I never got to meet the boss man.'

'Francine…' Angie eyed her friend with deep exasperation. 'Can't you see there's a big down side to this scheme? Guys who might not take no for an answer. I was lucky that Hugo Fullbright was gentleman enough not to really come on to me.'

'I can handle it.' Francine's grey eyes flashed reckless determination. 'And let me tell you if Hugo Fullbright is all you say he is, I would have been off to Tokyo with him like a shot. You've got to seize the main chance, Angie, make it work for you. That's how it is out there. You've been safely ensconced with Paul so long, you've got blinkered eyes.'

'Paul…' Angie's inner tension geared up several notches at the reminder of her long-term relationship which could very well be in serious jeopardy. She should have been worrying about it instead of…

'He wouldn't have seen the billboard, Angie,' Francine offered in anxious hope. 'Not travelling from his apartment at Woolloomooloo to the law court at Darlinghurst.'

Angie shook her head. 'It doesn't have to be Paul. Can you really imagine that not one of his friends or colleagues, having known us as a couple for years…not one of them would have driven across the Sydney Harbour Bridge this morning without noticing the billboard and recognising *Foxy Angel* as me?'

'It *is* possible,' Francine argued. 'I mean…they wouldn't be expecting it to be you.'

'Hugo Fullbright took one look at me—one look— and had no trouble whatsoever in making the connection.'

'But anyone who knows you—really knows you— would think they're mistaken. You're so straight, Angie. It's not your kind of thing at all.'

Why did that suddenly make her feel she'd lived her life in a straitjacket, limiting her options instead of expanding her horizons?

Francine rushed into apology again. 'I'm sorry. Truly, truly, sorry. If it causes trouble with Paul, just lay all the blame on me, where it belongs, and I'll tell him so myself. I won't mind if he considers me a hopelessly ditzy woman who doesn't know which side is which.'

That wasn't going to help. Paul would be furious. Mistake or not, he'd find the whole photo thing offensive.

'Surely he's big enough to laugh it off,' Francine suggested tentatively.

More likely he'd drag it into the law court, demanding redress. Though that could turn into a distasteful circus. Possibly he would choose to laugh it off on the principle of least said, soonest mended.

'We'll cross that bridge when we come to it,' Angie said on a helpless sigh. Her own state of confusion about how she felt towards Paul—and Hugo Fullbright—was making her stomach churn.

'Right!' Francine clearly hoped for a reprieve on the Paul front. 'So…ummh…was there any business in the meeting with Hugo Fullbright?' she asked warily. 'I mean…this didn't have some negative effect, did it? The contract is watertight.'

'We have his full approval to go ahead with our concept.'

'Great!' Huge relief.

Angie wished she could feel relief. The next best thing was distraction. 'Let's get to work, Francine.'

They worked.

Every time the telephone rang, Francine pounced

on it, anxious to divert any possible trouble from Angie. At lunchtime she offered to go to the local delicatessen to buy them both salads, thus avoiding the chance that Angie might be accosted by some guy wanting *Foxy Angel* to fulfil his fantasies.

It was a very special salad—Thai beef with mango. Angie's favourite.

Except her stomach was in no condition to appreciate it. She wondered if sushi would be easier to swallow, then wrenched her wayward mind off Tokyo and Hugo Fullbright and determinedly shoved lettuce leaves into her mouth.

The telephone rang.

Angie's stomach knotted up even further as she listened to Francine rattling out what had happened with the billboard, pulling out all stops to explain the mistake. It had to be Paul calling. And the way Francine was wilting was warning enough that he was not amused. Having exhausted all avenues of appeasement, she limply passed the receiver over, grimacing defeat.

'Paul…demanding to speak to you.'

Angie took a deep breath. 'Paul…'

'Our relationship is over!'

Just like that!

Not even a stay of judgement.

Angie was totally poleaxed, speechless.

'I can no longer afford to have you at my side,' he ranted on. 'I have been subjected to intolerable comments and sniggers from my colleagues all morning…'

'But…it's not my fault,' she managed to get out.

'Irrelevant!' he snapped. 'I do not intend to spend my time trying to explain away a mistake that no one will believe anyway. I've told people I severed our relationship last weekend and if you have any decency at all, you will back that up. If asked. The only saving grace from this mess is that I didn't go to the ballet with you last night. Goodbye, Angie.'

The line was disconnected before she could say another word.

The shock of this—this brutal dismissal from his life—stirred a turbulent anger that broke every restraint Angie would normally keep on her temper. She rose to her feet, marched over to Francine's desk and slammed the receiver down on the phone set, startling her friend into looking agog at her.

'What…what happened?' she asked nervously.

Angie ungritted her teeth and bit out, 'He dumped me.'

'He…' Francine swallowed hard. '…dumped you?'

'Three years together and he shoves me out in the cold, just like that!' Angie snapped her fingers viciously, growing more and more inflamed by the injustice of it all.

'I'll go and grovel to him, Angie. I'll…'

'Don't you dare!'

'But…'

'If Paul Overton came crawling to me on his hands and knees I wouldn't take him back,' Angie hurled at her, wheeling away and tramping around the office, working off a surge of violent energy and venting her ever-mounting outrage. 'It shows how much he cared about me. No love. No loyalty. No taking my side. Just wiping me off as though I was too tainted for him to touch anymore.'

She scissored a furious gesture at Francine who

was all galvanised attention. 'Even a criminal gets to have extenuating circumstances taken into consideration. And I'm innocent. Completely innocent.'

'You're right,' Francine gravely agreed. 'He doesn't deserve you.'

'He even backdated our separation to last weekend so he could save his precious pride in front of his precious colleagues, distancing himself from any action I've taken since then.'

'Mmmh…I wonder if he told them this was your revenge for being…'

'Francine!' Angie yelled in sheer exasperation.

It rattled her into trying to excuse her speculative mind-frame. 'I was just working it through…'

'I didn't do it, remember?'

'Completely and utterly innocent,' came the emphatic agreement. 'Uh…there's someone at the door, Angie,' she quickly added with the harried air of one wanting to grasp any distraction.

Angie swung to confront the intruder.

It was a florist delivery boy, carrying in a spectacular arrangement of exquisite orchids. He paused, glancing inquiringly from one to the other.

'Miss Angie Blessing?'

'That's me,' Angie snapped, eyeing him balefully. At this point in time, no male could be trusted.

'These are for you.'

'Fine. Thank you.'

She waved in the direction of her desk. He set the delivery down and scooted, undoubtedly aware that he'd blundered into an area mined with highly volatile sensibilities.

Angie glared at the gift.

Who would be sending her flowers?

Extremely expensive flowers.

There hadn't been time for Paul to start regretting his decision. If he ever did.

It was a very artistic arrangement, Japanese in style. This latter thought put a tingling in Angie's spine. It drove her over to the desk to unpin the attached note and read it.

A taste of Tokyo—Hugo.

The dark place in Angie's soul unfurled to a lovely blast of light. Hugo Fullbright didn't think she was too tainted to have at his side. He wanted her there. And he really valued her company. These perfect orchids had definitely cost him a small fortune.

'Right! I'm going!'

'Going where?' Francine asked in bewilderment.

'To Tokyo. With Hugo Fullbright.' She headed around the desk to get her handbag where she'd stowed his card.

Francine rocketed to her feet. 'Angie…Angie…just hang on a minute. This isn't a decision you should rush into.'

'Why not? You said yourself you'd go with him. Seize the main chance.' She found the card and held it triumphantly aloft as she moved to the telephone, abandoning all sense of caution on this wild plunge into a different future.

'It's not your style,' Francine argued frantically.

'And where did that get me? Dumped. Cast off. Devalued to nothing. This is the new me, Francine, and nothing you say is going to stop me.'

'But…'

'Not another word. I'm going.'

She snatched up the receiver and stabbed out the numbers printed on the card for Hugo Fullbright's

personal mobile telephone. Francine sank back onto
her chair, rested her elbows on the desk and covered
her face with her hands, emitting a low groan denot-
ing inescapable disaster. The buzzing call signal in
Angie's ear drowned out the mournful noise.

'Hugo Fullbright.' The name was rolled out in a
deep sexy voice.

Angie's stomach curled. She screwed it to the stick-
ing point. 'It's Angie Blessing. I've changed my
mind.'

'A woman's prerogative,' he said charmingly.

'The flowers are truly lovely.'

'They reminded me of you. Beautiful, appealing,
with a fascinating hint of the exotic.'

Angie's pulse rate accelerated but she determinedly
kept her voice calm. 'Thank you.'

'Our flight to Tokyo leaves at ten-thirty tomorrow
morning,' he went on matter-of-factly. 'I'll have my
chauffeur call for you at nine.'

His chauffeur. That was one up on Paul. Not that
she cared about Paul anymore. Not one bit!

'Can you be ready by then?'

A reminder that she'd been late for their meeting
this morning. 'Yes,' she said firmly. 'I'm not normally unpunctual.'

'Good! Now I do need your home address.'

She gave it.

'I'm very glad you changed your mind, Angie.' He
was back to purring.

Her heart started hammering. She told herself that
having the very personal attention of a jungle cat
would certainly broaden her horizons, not to mention
tripping off to Tokyo. It was time to live dangerously.
And best not to let Hugo Fullbright know there was

any apprehension in her mind. He was thinking *Foxy Angel*—bold and enterprising.

'I look forward to seeing you tomorrow, Hugo,' she said, deciding that was a reasonably foxy reply.

'Until tomorrow.' The purr positively throbbed with pleasurable anticipation.

Angie quickly put the receiver down. 'Done!' she said, not allowing the slightest quiver of doubt to shake her resolution.

Francine dragged her hands down enough to look at her with huge, soulful eyes. 'Please...please... don't blame me.'

'What for? I'm grateful to you, Francine. You showed Paul up for what he was.'

'A skunk,' she said with feeling.

'Absolutely. You saved me from wasting more time on him, liberating me so I can take a step in a new direction.'

'But is this direction right for you, Angie?' she worried.

'Won't know until I'm in Tokyo.' She grinned at Francine as she collected her handbag, wanting to show there would be no hard feelings between them, whatever the outcome of this adventure with Hugo Fullbright.

'Angie, you shouldn't think of it as a dirty weekend,' Francine anxiously advised.

Seeing her friend's genuine concern, Angie paused to give her the real truth. 'I don't care, Francine. Hugo really got to me this morning—made me wish I wasn't with Paul. I want to take this chance with him. Come what may.'

'You're not flying off the rails because of what Paul's done?'

Angie took a deep breath and slowly shook her head as she examined her feelings with absolute honesty. 'I'm so mad at Paul because I'm angry with myself for staying with him for so long. I knew it wasn't right. And I knocked Hugo back this morning because of him. I knocked him back and I'm not going to knock him back again. Paul never really focused on me. Hugo...' The sheer magnetism of the man tugging on her—just the thought of being with him tugging on her. '...he's something else, Francine, something I want to be part of, and now that I'm free of any sense of loyalty to Paul, I'm seizing this chance!'

Angie grabbed the arrangement of beautiful, exotic orchids and sailed out of the office, determined on pursuing this course of action wherever it led. She was thirty years old with nothing to lose. Hugo Fullbright beckoned very brightly—the man himself, the trip to Tokyo, the flowers, the chauffeur... all making her feel this might very well be the trip of a lifetime.

She wanted to go with him.

And go she would.

CHAPTER FOUR

HUGO FULLBRIGHT put away his mobile phone and relaxed back into the plush leather seat of his Bentley, grinning from ear to ear, enjoying his triumph. 'I won, James,' he said to the man driving him to his next meeting. '*Foxy Angel* is mine.'

'Congratulations, sir. Though I had no doubt you would win, once you set your mind on it.'

Hugo laughed, brimming over with good humour. He had to hand it to James. As his household executive, the man was brilliant. Only twenty-seven when Hugo had hired him four years ago—a New Age butler trained to do whatever was required of him: chauffeuring his boss, shopping, doing household chores, cooking, serving meals, co-ordinating the social calendar, making travel arrangements.

All that on top of the traditional trimmings—the art of etiquette, protocol, wine appreciation. Not to mention also being equipped with computer skills and having experience in conflict resolution.

Certainly James Carter was one of his best acquisitions, highly efficient and wonderfully discreet. He made the perfect confidant for Hugo because he was privy to all his affairs, both business and personal, and could be trusted with anything. Of course, he was paid very well, as befitting a top executive, and to Hugo's mind, he was worth every cent of his six-figure annual salary, plus perks.

Life moved very smoothly with James handling all

the details. Hugo appreciated that. So what if the guy was gay! Probably better that he was. James' mind was definitely on his job. A man's man. One hundred per cent. And like many gay guys, he had a great eye for stylish clothes, a great eye for everything.

Hugo knew that his suitcase would be perfectly packed ready for him to leave for Tokyo tomorrow morning, and best of all, Angie Blessing was going with him. 'You should see her in the flesh,' he said, the pleasure of it rolling through his voice as he remembered the amazing physical impact she'd had this morning. 'Well, you will see her.'

'Nine o'clock tomorrow morning,' James affirmed. 'I've written down the address.'

'Sex on legs...'

'You do seem to fancy legs, sir. All those models you've dated.'

Hugo frowned. The comparison was wrong. 'Angie Blessing is blessed with everything. Brains as well as beauty,' he corrected.

In fact, she put Chrissie Dorrington so far in the shade, on every count, he wished he'd met Angie long before this.

'Sounds like you might have hit the jackpot, sir.'

He might very well have. He could hardly wait to have his *Foxy Angel* to himself tomorrow. 'Thank you for finding the right florist, James,' he said appreciatively.

'Did the trick, sir?'

'A timely piece of persuasion.'

'If I may say so, sir, your timing is always impeccable. It's a pleasure to work for you.'

'Thank you.'

James was pleased everything had turned out well. He absolutely adored working for Hugo Fullbright. Not only was his employer suitably wealthy—cost no object with anything to do with his private life—but he had a flamboyant personality, never stuffy or boring. There was always something *happening*. It made life interesting, exciting, challenging.

And he was generous. Not a mean bone in his body. Generous with praise, and best of all, generous in showing his appreciation financially. James knew there wasn't a butler in Sydney with a higher wage than his.

Some of the rather peevish older butlers did not consider Hugo Fullbright *a gentleman*. He was one of the new rich, a racy bachelor, not really respectable. A bunch of bloody snobs, James thought, probably eaten up with envy. For one thing, they had to drive around in black Daimlers or silver grey Rolls-Royces, some even in an ordinary Mercedes. *He* had charge of a brilliant red Bentley. Mega-dollars with panache! No one could beat that!

All the same, James did feel it was time for his employer, who was now thirty-eight, to get married and have children. It would round off his life. James' life, as well. He'd been trained to look after kids and since it was most unlikely he'd ever have any of his own, there was no doubt in his mind that Hugo Fullbright's children would be fun. Definitely entertaining little creatures. How could they not be?

It would be very interesting to meet *Foxy Angel* tomorrow. Miss Blessing surely had a flamboyant personality, as well, or she wouldn't have put herself up on that billboard. This could be the perfect match.

James started planning what he'd pack for Tokyo.

The new Ian Thorpe brand underpants—very sexy—the Armani suit for dinner engagements—smooth sophistication—the Calvin Klein jeans for sightseeing—brilliant for showing off a taut, cheeky butt—the Odini black leather battle-jacket—some women were kinky for leather...

Ah, yes! If Miss Blessing was *the one*...still, it wasn't up to him. He'd do his bit to aid the process, should she be good enough for his boss. The billboard act *was* a bit dodgy. He'd know better tomorrow.

CHAPTER FIVE

THE doorbell rang at precisely nine o'clock.

Angie was ready. At least she was ready to go. She wasn't sure she was ready for this new situation with Hugo Fullbright—there was a swarm of butterflies in her stomach—but she'd weather it somehow and hopefully come up smiling. Which reminded her to put a smile on her face as she opened the door, starting off as she meant to go on, all bright and breezy.

'Good morning,' she lilted, determined that it would be good.

A surprisingly young man in a smart grey chauffeur's uniform tipped his cap to her while his eyes made a swift appraisal of his boss's new woman. Angie tensed, wondering if she passed muster. While it was summer in Australia, it was winter in Japan, so she'd teamed fine black wool pants with a frayed edge cropped jacket in black chenille, the latter very form-fitting with a diagonal hook and eye opening down the front which left a hint of cleavage on show, but not too much. Looking *foxy* wasn't really her style.

The chauffeur apparently approved, beaming a cheery smile right back at her. 'Good morning to you, Miss Blessing. My name is James Carter, answering to James.' He gestured to her suitcase and carry-on bag over which she'd slung her faux-fur leopard print overcoat, deciding it was definitely appropriate for wearing in the company of a jungle cat. 'Ready for me to take?'

'Yes. Thank you, James.'

'If you don't mind my saying so, Miss Blessing, I do like Carla Zampatti clothes. Always that subtle touch of class,' he said as he set about collecting her luggage.

Angie was so amazed at having the designer of her outfit recognised she barely got out another, 'Thank you.'

It dawned on her that the chauffeur was gay, which amazed her even further. The very macho Hugo Fullbright with a gay chauffeur? Well, why not? If he could pick a woman from a billboard photo, the man clearly had eclectic tastes in the people he drew into his life.

She didn't have to say goodbye to Francine who had left for work half an hour ago, squeezing Angie's hands as she said, 'Please…if things go wrong…just don't blame me.'

Angie would have much preferred a cheerful 'Good luck!' She was nervous enough as it was about what she was doing.

James led her down to the street where a gleaming red Bentley stood waiting. A red Bentley with cream leather upholstery! This was travelling in a style Angie had never experienced before. It made her feel like royalty, sitting in the back seat of such a car. The smile on her face did not have to be forced one bit.

Magnificent flowers.

Magnificent car.

Would the man match up to them?

And if he did, could she keep him?

She would hate it if she discovered that dirty weekends were his style when it came to women, picking them up and putting them down at his leisure, easy come, easy go. If he gave one hint of that she would not take the flight to Japan. She hoped it was an irresistible impulse on his part, as it was on hers.

'Will Mr. Fullbright be meeting me at the airport, James?' she asked, once they were on their way.

'We'll be picking him up from the Regent Hotel, Miss Blessing. He has a business breakfast there this morning. It was scheduled a week ago,' came the obliging information and explanation for his absence from her side.

'Thank you.'

A very busy man. And this trip to Tokyo had a business connection, as well. Angie wondered if he had room in his life for a wife and children. Not so far, and she judged him to be in his late thirties. Or maybe he was divorced. A bad marriage record. She needed to find out these things, though that kind of thinking was probably leaping too far ahead.

They drove over the harbour bridge. Angie checked the billboard, needing to know if her photo had been removed. She breathed a huge sigh of relief when she saw that Francine's image had replaced hers, then barely smothered a groan as she read the new caption—*Hot Chocolate.* Francine would have men's fantasies zooming!

Still, how could she criticise?

Foxy Angel had caught Hugo Fullbright's interest. Though that was a double-edged sword. Angie didn't know if he was genuinely attracted to her or caught up in a fantasy that appealed to him.

James used the car phone to alert his boss to their imminent arrival at the Regent Hotel. Running to schedule was clearly an important issue to such a busy man. Every minute counted. In fact, as the Bentley pulled up at the main entrance to the hotel, Hugo Fullbright was making his exit. Perfect timing.

Angie barely had a minute to compose herself before James was holding the passenger door open, and the man she was committed to spending the next three days with swept into the car, filling it with a vibrant energy. He flashed his white wolf smile at her and her heart hopped, skipped and jumped all over the place.

'Hi!' he purred, his eyes gobbling her up.

Angie knew the Bentley was air-conditioned but it suddenly felt very hot in there. 'Hi to you, too,' she replied with as much aplomb as she could muster. He was also wearing all black, a superbly tailored suit, silk shirt, and no tie. She found her gaze glued to the bared little hollow at the base of his throat until he spoke again.

'You look ravishing.' He rolled the R and Angie couldn't help feeling it was like a drum-roll anticipating many hours of ravishment.

Her toes curled.

'I was trying for beautiful, appealing, and exotic,' she tossed back at him.

He laughed. It was a laugh of pure enjoyment and Angie thought this weekend might be a lot of fun with him, if she could just let her hair down and go with it. For a long time there hadn't been any real fun with Paul. It was well past time she enjoyed life again, though she hoped for much more than a quickly passing enjoyment with Hugo.

The Bentley was in motion again, carrying her off with this man on very possibly the adventure of a lifetime—one that might lead to a lifetime of adventure! Maybe that was a hopeless fantasy but Hugo Fullbright certainly inspired it.

'Did your business breakfast go well?' she asked, interested in how he spent his time.

'A group of investors wanting to be in on my next property development. I'll let them know.' He reached over and took her hand, his thumb lightly fanning her skin again, sending electric tingles up her arm. 'I want to forget business now and learn more about you.'

Changing rooms.

'Is that how you manage your life, Hugo?' Angie asked curiously. 'Switching from one room to another? No cross-overs?'

'I don't want to bore you,' he purred, giving her the full riveting focus of his bedroom blue eyes.

Which was very flattering, having all his attention concentrated on her. Angie didn't know why she felt it was a smoke haze designed to keep her distant from the man behind the sexy charm, but her instincts demanded she challenge him.

'You think I'm some dumb blonde to be buttered up for her bed-worthiness?'

A sound suspiciously like a snort of amusement came from the driver's seat.

'Now how could I think that, Angie, when I'm trusting you with a huge budget to deliver the perfect finish for my apartments?' Hugo smoothly challenged back. 'I merely thought we could both take time out from work for a while. Enjoy each other's company without business intruding.'

'Fine! Just so you know I want to learn more about you, too.' And she gave him a long penetrating look to emphasise her interest was not purely sexual, nor centred on her own desirability to him.

He grinned. 'Well, I'd have to say I'm already flattered by the removal of your photo from the billboard.'

Heat scorched her cheeks. She barely bit back the impulse to state the truth again, which, of course, was *the straight* thing to do. And where would that get her? The sure knowledge that he wouldn't believe her anyway held her tongue. Her mind frantically composed a *foxy* reply.

'It seemed the decent thing to do since I'm not available...until further notice.'

Which put him on trial, competing for her interest. Best for him not to think she'd wiped every other guy out because he'd stepped forward. She'd had quite enough of the male ego from Paul Overton. No way was she going to let Hugo Fullbright think he could take her for granted because he considered himself so great!

He weighed her reply, his dynamite eyes twinkling appreciation of it. 'A move I respect,' he said. 'Thank you for giving me pole position. I promise I'll do everything in my power to ensure you won't regret it.'

And the power was coming at her in huge swamping waves. Angie just managed to collect her wits enough to continue the conversation. 'Interesting that you should use a car-racing term...pole position...and here you are with a very sedate Bentley.'

His brows drew together in mock disappointment. 'You don't like this car?'

'I love it. I'm just wondering why you chose it.'

'Can't I love it, too?'

'I would have thought a red Ferrari more your style. Dashing, glamorous, powerful...'

Something dark flickered in his eyes. 'No, I'm not into sports cars.' His mouth tilted sardonically. 'I wouldn't want any woman to think I'm the kind of man who needs one to make him a desirable male.'

Intriguing that he was touchy on the point. 'So the Bentley is...a perverse choice?' Angie queried, trying to probe for more.

'No.' He shrugged. 'It's simply *my* choice. A positive liking, not a negative reaction to something else.'

'They say a car does reflect the character of the man who owns it,' she mused, thinking of Paul with his Mercedes sports convertible—an establishment car with macho appeal.

'Tell me what this car stands for to you?' Hugo inquired, amused by the idea of testing her theory.

Angie paused to think about it, intuitively knowing her answer would be important in his judgement of her. 'Firstly, it yells very solid wealth. But also seriously classy style. Not something transient. It's the kind of car you could own all your life without its ever going out of style or losing its impact. Yet the red says its owner is not conservative. It's a bold choice, probably expressing his nature. I also think it's a statement that he doesn't care what other people think. Yet the high respectability of the car reassures them he can be trusted to deliver the goods, whatever they are.'

He nodded thoughtfully. 'An interesting analysis.' His mouth quirked. 'So you think I'm bold.'

Considering his blitzkrieg approach to her— 'Very,' she said with feeling.

'And you like that?' His eyes were twinkling teasingly again.

Angie's chest tightened up. Thoughts of sharing a bed with him—being bold—whizzed around her mind. 'It's...different,' she finally choked out.

He lifted her hand to his lips and pressed a very sensual kiss on her palm, his eyes never leaving hers as he did it. *'Vive la différence,'* he murmured with that throbbing purr of anticipation in his voice humming along every nerve in Angie's body.

She didn't even notice the Bentley slowing to a halt.

'Airport, sir,' James announced from the front seat.

'So...we begin our journey together,' Hugo said, still with the eye-lock that pinned Angie to her decision, despite the reality of the situation rushing in on her.

James was out of the car, holding the door open for them to alight. Hugo did not release her hand. He swung himself out and drew Angie after him. She arrived on the pavement adjacent to the international departure entrance, completely breathless and acutely aware of the man holding her.

Was she ready to go with him...accepting everything it entailed?

Was she really?

This was the moment of truth.

She could cry off, ask James to drive her back home again or get a taxi, cut every personal connection to the man. It was a woman's prerogative to change her mind. She could still do it. How was it going to feel right if she was just giving in to...*lust?*

Hugo was having no trouble with it. But men didn't, did they? They just followed their natural an-

imal instincts. It was only women who wanted more.
And she did want more than just sex. He was an
amazingly attractive, fascinating man. But if she
turned away from him now, what were the chances
he would pursue his current interest in her? He'd admired her sheer nerve in putting her face on a billboard! Wimping out of the weekend might completely wipe out his interest in her.

Hugo Fullbright was a bold man looking for a bold
partner. She could regret being bold, but wouldn't she
always regret not being bold? A man like him might
only come her way once in a lifetime.

Seize the main chance!

She didn't realise she'd squeezed his hand until he
shot her a quizzical glance. 'Nervous?'

'A bit!' she admitted. 'It's just hit me that I'm actually going to Tokyo with you.'

He flashed her a reassuring grin. 'I'll look after
you, Angie. I've been there before. Don't worry about
it.'

It wasn't the foreign country angle that was worrying her. However, she'd fretted away enough
minutes for James to have acquired a luggage trolley
and stacked everything ready to go. There it was in
front of them, Hugo's bags and hers, about to be con-
signed to a Qantas jet that would fly them both to
Japan.

Francine's advice slid into her mind—*You
shouldn't think of it as a dirty weekend.*

'I won't,' she said decisively.

'Good!' Hugo approved, thinking she was answering him.

James handed Angie her coat and tipped his cap.

'I hope you have a splendid journey, Miss Blessing,' he said chirpily.

'Thank you.'

He turned to Hugo. 'And you, sir, all the best! I'll check with the airport for your landing time on Monday morning.'

'Do that, James,' he said dryly. 'You might also need to see a doctor about your nose.'

'My nose, sir?'

'I've never heard you snort before.'

'I do beg your pardon, sir.' He frowned apologetically. 'A temporary ailment. I'll see to it.'

'Try to get it fixed before Monday morning.'

'You can count on it, sir.'

'I'm sure I can. Thank you, James.'

The chauffeur actually clicked his heels before turning away to round the Bentley, heading back to his driver's seat.

Hugo was smiling in some private amusement as he took charge of the luggage trolley. 'Nice coat,' he remarked, nodding to the leopard faux-fur hanging over her arm.

'I thought you'd like it,' she said, resolutely banishing any quiver from her legs as she walked at his side into the departure hall.

'Is that another piece of character analysis?' he asked in teasing challenge.

She shot him a foxy glance. 'You remind me of a jungle cat.'

'Ah! Survival of the fittest?'

'Slightly more dangerous than that.'

He laughed, making Angie's mind fizz with what might very well be dangerous pleasure.

But she wouldn't worry about that anymore.

It was not going to be a dirty weekend.

She refused to even think it might be that for him. It was going to be a getting-to-know-you fun weekend.

Wild, probably irresponsible, but didn't every woman deserve to just let her hair down and go with the flow without worrying about consequences for just a little while? Angie reasoned she could be sane and straight again when she came home. Until then she'd ride along on Hugo Fullbright's wave and if he dumped her at the end of it…well, at least she wouldn't be wasting three years on him.

CHAPTER SIX

HUGO decided he should probably try to get some shut-eye himself. They were four hours into their nine-hour flight to Tokyo and it would inevitably be a late night with his Japanese hosts once they arrived. Angie was out like a light, stretched out comfortably on the almost horizontal bed set up by the handy controls on their first-class seats.

He smiled over her apology for her drowsiness—the champagne on boarding the plane, the wines accompanying a very fine lunch, not much rest last night. He didn't mind. Her uninhibited pleasure in travelling first-class, happily accepting everything offered, enjoying it, had made it a delight to be with her, and gave him cause to reflect that too many of his companions in recent years had been picky women, demanding special food and drinking only mineral water on flights.

Not that he'd minded that. It was sensible to drink water and faddy diets seemed to be all the rage these days, but it was infinitely more companionable to have a woman with him who shared his lust for every pleasure in life.

Maybe the difference came from Angie's background. As with himself, there'd been no family wealth behind her. She'd climbed her own ladder, just as he had. Her parents had been flower children, and even now lived in an alternative society community up near Byron Bay, selling their arts and crafts to tourists.

Career-wise she'd well and truly earned her success, having the guts to get out on her own and capitalise on her talent for design, not riding on the back of anyone else. No doubt there would have been years of tight budgeting. That had to give an extra edge to enjoying the best of everything now. It did for him.

His own parents had chosen to live up on the North Coast, too—Port Macquarie, where he'd built them a retirement home with every luxury he could provide. They were happy there, and he dropped in on them when he could. Their only current concern was he hadn't found a nice girl and settled down to produce grandchildren for them.

Could Angie be the *nice* girl?

Hugo was bemused by the thought. He really had no yen to settle down. He liked his life just the way it was. Besides, he didn't need a wife. James ran a household probably better than any woman could. And Hugo was never short of feminine company when he wanted it.

Although…there was the matter of quality versus quantity. There were certainly qualities in Angie Blessing that lifted her…but this was only the beginning of their relationship. Far too soon to make a judgement, especially when it came to marriage.

Even more especially when it came to having children, which was the biggest responsibility of all. Possibly he would want them someday, but that could wait. He had no biological clock ticking. Besides, he'd want to get married first, and basically, he didn't trust any woman enough to hand her that much power over his life.

Angie's remark about sports cars had reminded him of Paul Overton, his arch-rival at school. The guy had been born with everything—good looks, brains, strong athletic ability, *and* a silver spoon in his mouth, the son and heir of a very wealthy establishment family with connections in the top legal and political circles. But that wasn't enough for Paul. He had to be number one at everything and it had always rankled him when Hugo pipped him for some prize or other.

And there was definitely no accident about the revenge he'd taken for those slights to his overweening ego. Being given a Porsche on his eighteenth birthday had handed him the tool to snag Hugo's girlfriend, and he'd deliberately set out to do it. Right in front of him. With smug triumph.

The guy was a top barrister now, probably manoeuvring his way towards a seat in parliament. If he ever made it to Prime Minister, Hugo sure as hell wasn't going to vote for him. But Paul had inadvertently taught him a lesson about women. They were inevitably drawn to what looked like the higher prize. And these days, if the prize didn't live up to their expectations of happily married life, there was always the divorce settlement to look forward to.

No thanks.

He'd worked too hard, risked too much, won too many battles to hand over half the spoils to a woman who'd done nothing to contribute to them. He was quite happy to share them, as with Angie here and now, as long as he had the controlling hand.

Even with Angie, whom he found so very appealing on many levels…would she have come with him on this trip if he wasn't a top runner in the wealthy bachelor stakes? If he hadn't sent her flowers that few men could afford, reinforcing what was on offer? He'd certainly won her, but had he won her because the price was right?

Irrelevant really. He had her with him, which was what he'd wanted. And she hadn't done any running after him, actually backing off when he'd offered himself, certainly not leaping at the invitation. At least, she'd provided him with a challenge—quite a rare event—and while she'd opened up a lot about herself since they'd been in flight, there was still something cagey about her, keeping a reserve while testing him out, as though there were other things more important to her than his surface attributes.

Foxy Angel….

Could be a lot of fun while it lasted, Hugo thought with much pleasurable anticipation, and pressed the controls to lower his seat into the bed position. Best that he be well rested for tonight, too. He wanted to enjoy every aspect of Angie Blessing, and be in top form to do precisely that.

A feather-light touch on her cheek tingled into Angie's consciousness, followed by the purring sound of Hugo Fullbright's voice.

'Wake up, sleeping beauty.'

No dream.

Her heart kicked out of its slumberous rhythm. Her eyes flew open. He was right next to her, instantly taking her breath away with his white wolf smile.

'We're about ninety minutes from Tokyo…'

She'd slept for hours!

'…and light refreshments are being served. Probably

best you eat something before we land. It will be a late dinner tonight,' he warned.

Angie bolted upright, a flood of embarrassment heating her face. 'I'm so sorry. I thought I'd only doze for a while.'

'No problem.' His grin was positively wicked. 'Nice to know you don't snore.'

Which turned up her temperature even more. 'I'll go and tidy up. Back in a minute.' She grabbed her handbag and scooted away, needing time out to regain her composure, not to mention urgent repairs to her make-up.

The reminder that she'd be *sleeping* with him to-night had completely flustered her again. She'd put it out of her mind once they'd boarded the plane, de-termined to focus on having fun and enjoying Hugo's company. And he'd let her do that, not pushing any-thing *physical,* happy to indulge her in a getting to know you conversation. It had made her feel com-fortable with him—as comfortable as she could be, given that he was a very sexy man and she was un-deniably excited by him.

Those dynamite blue eyes twinkling at her, warmly appreciative, admiring, teasing, laughing...above all, really interested in her. It hadn't felt like just a flir-tatious game, filling in time until he could pounce. It had felt...good. Very good.

Angie tried to wash the heat from her face with a thorough dousing of cold water. She was being silly, worrying about tonight. Hugo liked her. She could tell. And the liking was definitely mutual. Besides, if she wanted to say no, she was sure he would respect that. Her instincts told her he would turn away from forcing any woman to do what she didn't want.

A matter of pride.

Though he hadn't bragged about how clever he'd been in targeting the real estate market as a money-maker, starting off with buying and selling, building up funds so he could move into property development. She had virtually dragged the details out of him. His attitude had been more dismissive than proud.

Yet he was a self-made billionaire and Angie couldn't help but admire the enterprising way he'd achieved that. Nothing handed to him on a plate...unlike Paul. Though that was probably unfair. Paul wouldn't be where he was if he hadn't applied himself to using all his attributes very effectively. They were just different men, coming from different places.

Vive la difference...

She smiled over the phrase Hugo had used as she got out her make-up bag, needing to put on her best face for whatever was waiting for her in Tokyo.

It also made her feel good that Hugo hadn't looked down his nose at her parents' lifestyle or been critical of it in any way, musing that she must have had a free and happy childhood, allowed to pursue whatever interests she liked, no pressure to meet expectations.

He was the late and only child of more elderly parents, not pushy people either, but his achievements had given them a lot of pleasure and he liked doing things for them. Angie thought it was great that he'd built them a luxurious retirement home in the location of their choice. Definitely a loving son.

It was a warming thought to take back to her seat beside him, having restored her face to presentability and brushed her hair back into shape.

The cabin steward was hovering, waiting to serve the light refreshments. Her seat was upright again, the tray lifted out ready to be lowered. Angie quickly settled, apologising for the delay.

'There's no hurry. We have plenty of time,' Hugo soothed.

She flashed him a quick smile. He really was a nice man, though he was looking at her again as though he'd prefer to taste her rather than what the cabin steward was offering. It gave Angie goose bumps.

As soon as they were served, she opened up a conversation, desperately needing the distraction of talk to lessen the physical effect he had on her. 'Tell me about the people we're meeting tonight, Hugo. I'll probably need to practice their names so I'll get them right.'

He obliged her, describing the men and what positions they held, repeating their names until she'd memorised them and was pronouncing them correctly.

'Can you speak Japanese?' she asked, wondering if she was going to be a complete fish out of water at their dinner.

'Yes. I learnt it at school and have polished up my knowledge of it since then,' he answered matter-of-factly. 'But don't worry about a language barrier, Angie,' he hastened to add. 'Since we're their guests, they'll be speaking English.'

'Oh! Well, that's a relief.'

He laughed, his eyes caressing her with a warm approval that set her heart pitter-pattering. 'I'm glad you care enough to learn their names,' he remarked.

'It's only polite.'

'And good business.'

'I believe in being prepared.'

He cocked a wickedly challenging eyebrow at her. 'For everything?'

'I wasn't prepared for you,' she shot back at him.

He grinned. 'Taken by surprise. Jungle cats do that.'

Would he pounce before she could think? A primitive little thrill shocked her into wondering if she wanted that, wanted the responsibility of making the decision shifted off her shoulders. Her gaze dropped nervously to his hands. Somehow it reassured her that his fingernails were neatly manicured. He wouldn't be rough. Sleek and powerful. Her stomach contracted as she imagined him bringing those assets into play, but she wasn't sure if it was fear or excitement causing havoc with her inner muscles.

She forced her mind back onto safe ground. 'Since you can speak the language, would you please teach me the correct greeting and how to say thank you in Japanese?'

Again he obliged her, coaching her pronunciation as she practised the phrases, letting her become comfortable with the foreign words, amused by her satisfaction in being able to remember them and say them correctly. He made a light game of it, passing the time pleasantly until they landed at Narita Airport.

The business of disembarking and collecting their luggage made Angie very aware that she was now actually in Japan, with nothing familiar around her, and the only person who knew her here was Hugo Fullbright. It made her feel dependent on him, which was rather unsettling, but he smoothly took control of everything so she had nothing to worry about. Except how he might take control of her.

They were met by a smartly dressed chauffeur and Angie wondered why he was wearing white gloves, which stood out in stark contrast to his dark uniform. They were ushered to a gleaming black limousine. Along the top of the passenger seat was a spotless, and obviously freshly laundered white lace covering, precisely where heads might rest.

Angie looked curiously at it as she settled beside Hugo, prompting him to explain, 'The Japanese are big on hygiene. You'll find Tokyo a very clean city.'

Different culture, different customs, she thought, wondering what other surprises were in store for her.

Hugo took her hand, giving it a reassuring squeeze. 'You'll love it, Angie. Although it's too dark now for you to see, the overall impression of the city as you drive in is of a huge white metropolis. There aren't the masses of red roofs you see when flying over Sydney. Tokyo is the whitest city I've seen anywhere in the world.'

Of course he would notice that, being a property developer, Angie thought, but it was a fascinating fact to hoard in her mind, which was altogether too busy registering the sensations being stirred by his closeness to her, now that they were virtually alone together and he was holding her hand again.

Hugo continued to talk about features of the city as they were driven to their hotel, pointing out Disneyland as they passed it. She hadn't known there was one here. Nor had she known about the Tokyo Tower that was constructed similarly to the Eiffel Tower, only higher.

As a tour guide, Hugo added a great deal of interest to the trip, yet Angie was far more conscious of him as a man, and while he appeared perfectly relaxed, she sensed a simmering energy waiting for the right moment to burst into action.

Occasionally his gaze would drop to her mouth when she spoke back to him, watching the movement of her lips, as though imagining how they'd respond to his. There were flashes of dark intensity behind the sparkle in his eyes. The hand holding hers did not remain still, his fingers stroking, seemingly idly, yet to Angie's mind, with sensual purpose, stirring thoughts of how his touch would feel in other places. Sometimes he leaned closer to her, pointing something out, and the tantalising scent of some expensive male cologne accentuated his strong sexiness.

When they reached the Imperial Hotel, they were driven to the VIP entrance and met by a whole entourage of hotel management, everyone bowing to them, then taking charge of their luggage and escorting them along wide corridors, up in a classy elevator, right to the door of their suite and beyond it to ensure everything was to their satisfaction.

It was mind-boggling treatment to Angie. She'd imagined this kind of thing only happened to royalty or heads of state or famous celebrities. Was Hugo considered *a star* by the Japanese? She was certainly moving into a different stratosphere with him. This suite had to be at least presidential. The floral arrangements alone were stunning.

She was still trying to take it all in as Hugo chatted to their entourage and ushered them out, dealing smoothly with the situation as though he was born to it. Angie was way out of her depth, yet she couldn't deny it was an exhilarating experience to be given so much courtesy and respect. All because she was with *this man,* she reminded herself. It was enough to turn any woman's head.

As he walked back to where she stood, still dumbstruck by the extraordinary world she'd stepped into, Hugo gestured towards the bathroom and warned, 'We don't have a great deal of time before the call will come for us to be taken to dinner. Would you like to shower first?'

Angie nodded as a swarm of butterflies attacked her stomach again. Bathroom…naked…with him prowling outside in this very private suite.

'Let me take your coat.'

His hands were on the collar, drawing the coat off her shoulders, down her arms. He was standing so close, face to face, Angie's breath was helplessly trapped in her lungs. He tossed the coat on an armchair. Then his hands were sliding around her waist, his mouth smiling his wolf smile, his eyes sizzling now with sexual challenge.

'It feels I've been waiting a long time for this,' he purred, and Angie had a panicky moment at the thought of being devoured by him.

Yet as soon as his mouth claimed hers, she knew she'd been waiting for this, too, wanting to know how she'd feel when he kissed her, needing to know, hoping it would settle the questions that had been buzzing around in her mind. She slid her arms up around his neck, closed her eyes, let it happen, all her senses on extreme alert.

It didn't start with any marauding forcefulness, more a seductive tasting that charmed her into responding, sensual lips like velvet brushing hers and the electric tingling of his tongue gliding over them, inviting—inciting—her to meet it, to open up to him, to explore more.

A slow kiss, gathering an exciting momentum as Angie was drawn into a deeper, more intimate journey with him, and she felt the pressure of his hands, gathering her closer, bringing her into full body contact with him, gliding over her curves as though revelling in their soft femininity, loving it.

Somehow his touch gave her the sense of being intensely sexy, making her acutely aware that she certainly hadn't felt this desirable to Paul for a long time. Maybe it was simply the wild pleasure of finding this dangerous gamble with Hugo was stirring sensations that some primal need in her wanted in order to make the risk right. Angie's mind wasn't really clear on this as it was being bombarded by impressions of the hard, strong maleness of the man who was holding her, kissing her as though he was enthralled by what she was giving him.

Then all thought disintegrated as he kissed her a second time, her mouth totally engaged with his in an explosion of passion so invasive that her whole body yearned to be joined with his, and exulted in knowing he was similarly aroused, desire becoming a vibrant urgency that could not be ignored.

And to Angie's confusion afterwards, it was Hugo who backed away from it, not she. He moved gently, not abruptly, slowly lessening the white-hot ardour, disengaging himself, taking a deep breath. 'We don't have enough time, Angie,' he murmured, his voice uncharacteristically rough, strained. 'You'd better go and have your shower now.'

She went, though how her quivering legs carried her into the bathroom she didn't know. The image of herself in the vanity mirror seemed like that of a woman in a helpless daze. How could there be so much incredibly strong feeling coursing through her? She'd barely met Hugo Fullbright…and all her worry about saying no to him…while here she was with her whole body screaming yes.

Having managed to undress and cram her long hair into a shower cap, Angie turned on a blast of water and tried to wash herself back to normal. Conscious of time being in short supply, she didn't linger under the sobering spray, quickly drying herself and donning the bathrobe supplied by the hotel. Cap off, clothes scooped into her arms, and she was out of the bathroom, calling to Hugo, 'It's all yours.'

He'd stripped down to his underpants!

Her gaze instantly veered away from them, though she barely stopped herself from staring at the rest of his bared physique—more definitively muscular than Paul's, very powerful thighs, and smoothly tanned olive skin that gleamed as though it was polished. No hair at all on his chest. Somehow she forced herself to keep moving towards her suitcase which was set on a luggage stand, ready for her to open.

'Thanks,' he said, flashing her an approving smile for not holding them up too long as he headed for the bathroom.

Angie dressed as fast as she could, her heart pumping overtime as she castigated herself for comparing Hugo to Paul. Hugo Fullbright was his own man. Paul was gone from her life. It was just difficult to wipe three years out in what was little more than a day. Even more difficult to come to terms with the fact that she'd been intimate with one man last week and was now about to plunge into intimacy with another.

But she hadn't really been happy with Paul, she frantically reasoned.

And Hugo was…special.

Incredibly special.

It didn't matter how soon it was and how fast it was happening, not to admit she wanted him was stupid. Better to be *straight* with herself—and him—than play some *foxy* game that would leave them both frustrated. Games weren't her style. Never had been.

Though whether this relationship would have any future in it or not, she had no idea. Francine would think she was mad not to suss that out first, and she probably was mad. Maybe she'd have second thoughts about it all before they returned to the hotel after dinner.

She'd chosen her Lisa Ho outfit for tonight—crushed velvet in shades of green; a Chinese style jacket with long fitted sleeves flaring at the wrist, and a long slim-line skirt that flared gracefully below her knees. Black high heels with sexy crossover ankle straps. She'd just seated herself at the well lit dressing table to attend to her grooming when Hugo emerged from the bathroom, a towel tucked around his hips.

Angie's heart was already galloping. It positively thundered as he stripped off and set about dressing. He was not acting in any exhibitionist way, just going naturally about the business of putting his clothes on, perfectly comfortable with having a woman in the room with him, chatting to her as though everything was absolutely normal.

She couldn't help thinking he was used to these circumstances. Inviting a woman away for a weekend was probably as familiar to him as it was unfamiliar for her to accept such a proposition. Which begged the question—was she just one of a queue that suited him far more than any permanent relationship would? An endless queue of women he found desirable at the time, but who'd always have a *use by* date?

Angie wasn't happy with that thought.

Yet it seemed to fit.

He wasn't married.

He'd never been married.

The telephone rang—notification that their car had arrived.

Angie quickly grabbed her small evening bag and stood up, ready to go. Hugo put down the telephone receiver and his gaze swept her from head to foot, before lingering on the row of buttons fastening the front of her jacket. *He* was now dressed in a superb pin-striped navy suit, looking both moody and magnificent.

'Will I do in this outfit?' she asked nervously, willing her legs to get steady so she could walk safely in these precarious shoes.

His face lightened up as he smiled with a touch of irony. 'You do…extremely well…in every sense.'

Her whole body flushed.

'I'd have to say the same of you,' she tripped out, trying to keep a level head.

He laughed. 'Then we clearly make a fine couple.'

And Angie carried that wonderfully intoxicating thought with her as they started out for their first night in Tokyo.

CHAPTER SEVEN

HUGO found it difficult to keep his mind focused on appreciating the hospitality of his hosts, let alone pursuing their subtle interest in future business. Tonight he was definitely not on top of the game. In fact, he was seriously distracted by Angie Blessing.

He couldn't remember the last time he'd been so excited by a woman. His usual control had slipped alarmingly when he'd kissed her. He'd actually struggled to assert it again, having to fight his reluctance to part from her, despite the tight schedule that demanded other action. And even now the provocative row of buttons down the front of her jacket was playing havoc with his concentration.

Ironically enough, his hosts were charmed by her, as well. Maybe it was an innate business sense coming to the fore, or simply a genuine interest in them and their country, but she delighted them with the very positive energy she brought to this meeting. Hugo mentioned the work Angie was doing on his latest project and they presented her with their business cards and respectfully requested hers. She was definitely quite a hit with them, doing herself proud. And him.

He could not have chosen a better partner—he frowned over that word—*companion* for this weekend. Why had he thought *partner?* Angie Blessing had been very accurate in naming herself *Foxy Angel*. She was demonstrating that right, left and centre—

clever and beautiful. It was okay to admire her, want her in his bed, but it would be stupid of him to lose his objectivity with this woman. Bad enough that he was currently sucked in to thinking about her all the time.

No doubt that would change soon, Hugo assured himself.

Anticipation was insidious.

Satisfaction would put his mind back in order.

Angie's mind was dancing waltzes with Hugo Fullbright. A bridal waltz featured very strongly. Pure fantasy at this point, but it buoyed her spirits enormously to mentally see them as a well-matched *couple,* fitting perfectly together.

In every sense.

Not just sexual!

This dinner party was turning out to be very much a pointer in that direction, much to Angie's relief and delight.

Their Japanese hosts seemed to like her, even giving her their business cards. Not that she expected anything to come of their taking hers, but it was a mark of respect, and best of all, Hugo had talked up her talent for interior design, making the point that she was very successful in her area of expertise—an accolade that made her a focus of interest, as well as him.

His ego had not demanded she simply be an ornament on his arm, though it was his business that had brought him to Tokyo. To Angie, it was an amazing thing for him to do. She tried to return the favour by being as congenial a guest as it was possible for her to be.

Which wasn't difficult. She was truly having a marvellous time—dining in a private room in this obviously high-class Japanese restaurant. The walls were made of the traditional paper screens, lending a unique ambience, and while they did sit on cushions on the floor, luckily there was a pit under the table to accommodate legs—a concession for Westerners?

They were served by wonderfully graceful Japanese ladies dressed in kimonos, and each course of what seemed like a never-ending banquet was artfully presented. Much of the food Angie didn't recognise but Hugo helpfully explained what it was whenever she looked mystified. She was happy to try all the different tastes. The seaweed soup was the only course she couldn't handle. Three mouthfuls and her eyes were begging Hugo to be released from eating more.

He grinned and lifted his little cup of sake, indicating she could leave the soup and appreciate the rice wine instead. The sake was surprisingly good and Angie had to caution herself not to drink too much of it. Her level of intoxication was already incredibly high, just being with this man who made her feel valued and appreciated and understood.

Of course, he did want her, as well.

There was no ignoring what was all too evident in the way he looked at her whenever there was a lull in the conversation. It was a wonder the buttons on her jacket didn't curl right out of their eyelet fastenings from the searing intent in those bedroom blue eyes. Angie could feel her breasts tingling with a tight swelling in response and knew she wouldn't try to stop him from undressing her once they were alone in their suite again. The very thought of it excited her.

His hands, his mouth, his body, the kind of person he was...everything about him excited her. She felt as though all her lucky stars were lining up to deliver the best that life had to offer tonight. No way in the world could she turn her back on it.

The time finally came for them to take leave of their hosts. Angie found herself babbling in a kind of wildly nervous exhilaration during the limousine ride back to the hotel. Hugo was not nearly so verbose, patiently listening to her gush of pleasure in the marvellous evening.

Patiently waiting.

Making no move to pounce.

Waiting...waiting...

The reality of what was about to happen didn't really hit Angie until they were on their way up to their hotel suite, the elevator doors closed, locking them into the small compartment, no one else with them, alone together. The feeling that she was now cornered rushed in on her, choking her into silence.

She needed Hugo to say something light to break her tension, to ease her into the next inevitable step, to somehow make her more comfortable with the idea of *sleeping* with him, but he didn't. The hand holding hers gripped more tightly, as though affirming she was caught—no escape. And the waiting was almost over. A matter of minutes...seconds...and he'd have her exactly where he wanted her.

The elevator doors opened onto their floor. Her feet were drawn into matching his steps while her heart thumped a rapid drum-roll and her mind whirled like a dervish, wildly trying to rationalise the choice she'd made.

Hugo hadn't forced her into anything.

She was here of her own free will.

Wanted to be with him.

All she needed was for him to kiss her again.

It would feel all right then.

He opened the door to their suite, placed a hand at the pit of her back, gently nudging her forward, a guiding hand, perfectly civilised, not the paw of a panther poised for the kill. And she was not walking into a dark, dangerous jungle. He switched the lights on for her to see she was once again in luxurious surroundings.

The curtains had been closed, blocking out the night view of the city. The door behind her was closed. Rather than look at the bed which loomed too largely in her mind, Angie fastened her gaze on the magnificent floral arrangement gracing the coffee table in the lounge area.

Her shoulders were rigid when Hugo lifted her coat from them, removing it for her. It was no more than a gentlemanly courtesy. He didn't try to make it more. She fiercely told herself to relax but her body had gone completely haywire as she felt the heat of his nearness to her, smelled the cologne he used.

'Have I assumed too much, Angie?'

The loaded question snapped her into swinging around to face him. He'd tossed her coat aside and was unbuttoning his suit coat, but his eyes stabbed straight into hers, probing like twin blue lasers.

'What...' It was barely a croak. Her mouth was so dry she had to work some moisture into it before she could get out the words. '...what do you mean?'

A mocking glint challenged her as he bluntly stated, 'You're frightened.'

'No, I'm not,' she shot back at him, instinctively denying any form of cowardice.

His coat joined hers on the dividing bench between the bedroom and living areas. His eyes derided her assertion as he began undoing his tie. 'I've been with too many women not to know how it is when they're willing…and eager…to go to bed with me.'

'Maybe that's the problem…too many women,' she defended hotly. And truthfully, as the thought of being only one in an ongoing queue burst into her mind again.

His mouth tilted ironically. 'I'm not in my teens, Angie. Neither are you,' he added, hitting the raw place Paul's dumping had left.

'So I should know the score?' she retorted with a bitter note he instantly picked up on, his eyes narrowing, weighing what was behind the response.

Her cheeks burned with guilt and shame. Hugo had every right to assume what he had and it was terribly wrong of her to give him a negative reaction because of Paul. She wasn't being fair.

'I'm not into keeping scores,' he said with a careless shrug. The tie was tossed on top of the coats. He flicked open the top buttons on his shirt, then started removing the cufflinks from his sleeves, dropping his gaze to the task in hand.

The cufflinks were black opals, rimmed with silver. Angie watched his fingers working them through the openings, savagely wishing she'd kept her mouth shut.

'Nor am I into bed-hopping,' he went on matter-of-factly. 'Every woman in my life has had my exclusive attention until such time as the relationship broke down…for whatever reason.'

'Why did your last relationship break down?' The question slipped out before she could clamp down on it, curiosity overriding discretion.

His gaze flicked up as he slid the cufflinks into his shirt pocket. His eyes mocked her need to know as though it shouldn't be important to her. But he did answer her in a sardonic fashion. 'I caught Chrissie snorting cocaine. I'm not into drugs, either. She'd lied to me about staying off them.'

Chrissie… Her mind latched onto the name, though it meant nothing to her. Just as Paul would mean nothing to Hugo. A new relationship should start with a clean slate. Why was she messing this up?

Hugo turned away from her, moving over to the bed. 'What about you, Angie?' he tossed back over his shoulder. 'Do you need an artificial high to unleash yourself sexually?'

Contempt in his voice.

For her or for Chrissie? Angie took a deep breath, needing to recapture his respect. 'No, I don't. Nor would I want to stay involved with someone who used drugs.'

'Glad to hear it. Makes people unreliable.'

He sat on the end of the bed and started removing his shoes and socks, not the least bit perturbed about her watching him undress. Weirdly enough, Angie didn't feel in any way threatened by it. His detached manner seemed to place her on some outer rim, having no influence at all on what he did. Yet she knew intuitively he was very aware of her presence and he was waiting again, waiting for her to give him something to work with.

The problem was she couldn't make herself move. Any physical approach felt like a horribly false step, like throwing herself at him, which he'd surely view cynically at this point. And she couldn't think straight enough to know what would be the right thing to say.

He tucked his socks in his shoes—a tidy man who obviously preferred a *tidy* life—and sat upright, the expression on his face suggesting he'd been struck by an idea that he found oddly titillating.

'Are you a virgin, Angie? Is that why you're so nervous?'

'No!' The denial exploded from her, throwing her into more anguished confusion over what she should do to correct the negative impressions she hadn't meant to give this man, especially when he was the most attractive man she'd ever met.

He cocked his head consideringly. 'Have you been…attacked by a man?'

She shook her head, mortified that he should judge her as sexually scarred by a bad experience.

He stood up, casually rolling his flapping sleeves up his strong muscular forearms as he strolled back towards her. 'Are you worried about protection?' he inquired, frowning over her frozen attitude. 'If that's the case…' He paused, waving to the far bedside table. '…I did bring a supply of condoms with me. You have no need to fear unwelcome consequences.'

'Thank you,' she choked out, feeling an absolute idiot for getting herself into such an emotional tangle when he was being perfectly civilised and looking after everything like the gentleman he clearly was.

A wry little smile sat provocatively on his lips as he slowly closed the distance between them and lifted his hand to stroke his knuckles gently down her burning cheek. 'I'd have to say this is not what I expected of *Foxy Angel.*'

She wanted to say—*Just kiss me*—but what came blurting out of her mouth was, 'I'm not *Foxy Angel.*'

It shocked him into a freeze on action. 'Pardon?'

'*Foxy Angel* is *Hot Chocolate.*'

He shook his head as though she wasn't making sense.

'On the billboard this morning.'

'It was a different photo. Different woman.'

'Yes. It was the photo that should have been used yesterday with the caption of *Foxy Angel.* Francine had to change the name to something else to avoid confusion.'

'Francine...' Again he shook his head, not taking it in.

'I tried to explain to you at our meeting that a mistake had been made. You didn't want to believe me. But the truth is that my friend had sent in a photo of the two of us and the technician had used the wrong half. Francine is the one who's marketing herself.'

'This is absurd,' he tersely muttered.

'Worse than absurd,' she retorted heatedly, and before Angie could think better of them, more damning words tripped out. '*You* took the wrong impression of me, and my partner of three years was so humiliated by the billboard he dumped me cold.'

The cloud of irritation and confusion instantly dissipated. The air suddenly sizzled with electric energy as dangerous bolts of lightning were hurled at her from Hugo's eyes. 'So what is this? Your revenge on men?'

Her heart contracted under the violent force of his

reaction. A convulsive shiver ran down her spine. But her mind rose to the challenge, sharp and clear.

'No. I came with you because I wanted to. Because I'm attracted to you. But I've never done anything like this before and...'

'And you got cold feet,' he finished for her, the frightening electricity instantly lessening.

'Yes,' she admitted, sighing with relief at his quick understanding. 'I'm sorry. I didn't mean to be such a fool...' She gestured her inner anguish. '...when it came to this.' Her eyes begged his forgiveness. 'I knew what you expected...'

Hugo's mind was spinning, fitting all the odd pieces into this new picture of Angie Blessing, realising everything about her made better sense now. 'It's okay,' he quickly soothed, playing for time, needing to get the action right when he moved in on her.

No question that he had to if he was to be certain of keeping her, and keeping her was now his prime objective. He wanted this woman and it was abundantly clear that he had to make his claim tonight. Letting her off the hook would only give her more time to doubt her decision to come with him, more time to think about the guy who'd dumped her, perhaps wanting him back, hoping he would reconsider and call her on Monday.

The attraction she'd admitted to was real.

There'd been ample proof of that in the way she'd responded to him before they'd gone out to dinner.

Hugo could barely quell the raging desire to blot the other guy out of her mind. Gently, gently, he told himself. He'd never seduced a woman before—never had to—but if he had to seduce Angie Blessing, he would.

This woman was going to be his.

CHAPTER EIGHT

FRANCINE was right.

Dirty weekends weren't her style.

The relief at getting everything straight with Hugo was so enormous, Angie felt totally light-headed. Even her heart was skipping happily as though a terrible pressure had been lifted. Especially since Hugo had told her it was okay with him, accepting that he had been at fault, too, disbelieving her explanation of the mistake. Though she shouldn't have played up to the false identity. Any form of deception was wrong.

'I should have told you the truth before I accepted your invitation,' she said ruefully.

He smiled. Not his wolf smile. There was a warm caress in his eyes, making her feel better. 'I'll take that omission as a measure of your wanting to be with me,' he said, a hint of appeal taking the ego edge out of his statement.

'I did. I do,' she eagerly assured him.

'Then it's all good, Angie. Because if you had laid it out to me, I would still have pressed the invitation. *Foxy Angel* had its appeal but only because it was attached to you.'

She could feel herself glowing with pleasure.

It truly was okay.

Hugo was attracted to her, not some fantasy.

He tilted her chin, locking her gaze to the powerful intensity of his as he softly said, 'Believe me, the guy was a fool for letting you go. But I almost feel kindly towards him because he opened the door for me.'

His hand slid up over her cheek with a feather-light touch, the kind of reverent touch used in feeling something precious, wanting a tactile sense of what made it so special. Angie's breath caught in her throat and she stayed absolutely still, feeling thrilling little tingles spreading over her skin.

'And I now have enough time with you to show *I* value you,' he went on. 'Far more than he did.'

The purr of his voice was thrilling, too, not threatening at all. And what he was saying hit deep chords of truth. Paul hadn't valued her. He'd thrown her away like garbage, while Hugo treated her not only as an equal partner, but as a woman whose feelings really mattered to him.

'It's easy to get blinded by familiarity, Angie,' he murmured caringly. 'Not seeing what else there can be, only feeling safe with what you've known before. But I want you to look at me, feel how it is with me, give it a chance. Will you do that?'

'Yes…' She wanted to very much, was dying for him to kiss her as he had before.

He did.

Though so gently at first, it was even more tantalisingly sensual, giving her plenty of time to relax into the kiss, and Angie revelled in his obvious sensitivity to how she was reacting, responding. She understood he was exerting maximum control for her sake, wanting her to feel right with him, and this understanding removed any inhibition she might have had about moving closer to him, lifting her arms to wind them around his neck, inviting a deepening of the kiss, wanting to give as he was giving.

It was only fair.

Yet he seemed to shy away from trying to incite the passion he'd stirred before, his mouth leaving hers to graze around her face, planting warm little kisses on her temples and eyelids as his arms enclosed her in their embrace, one hand drawing its fingers slowly through her hair as though enjoying its silky flow around them.

'Everything about you feels good to me,' he murmured. 'Your hair...' He rubbed his cheek over it. '...your skin...' His lips trailed down her cheek to her ear which he explored very erotically with his tongue, arousing sensations that zinged along every nerve in Angie's body. '...the lovely soft curves of your body. All of you...beautiful,' he whispered, his breath as tingling as his tongue as he expelled warm air on a deeply satisfied sigh.

She couldn't even begin to catalogue his appeal to her. It was fast becoming totally overwhelming. Her mind was swimming in a marvellous sea of pleasure, revelling in his appreciation of her and loving his intense masculinity.

His fingers caressed the nape of her neck, slowly traced the line of her spine to the pit of her back. Then both his hands were gliding lower, gently cupping her bottom, subtly pressing her into a closer fit with him.

He was aroused.

Oddly enough, given her *cold feet,* it was not a chilling reminder that she was playing with fire, more a comforting reassurance that he really did desire the woman she was, a very warming reassurance that everything within her welcomed—more than welcomed when he kissed her again, not holding back this time, a long driving kiss that exploded into a passionate need to draw her into wanting all he could give her.

And Angie did want it.

It didn't matter that joining with this man might be premature, ill-considered, foolishly impulsive. She forgot all about being one of a queue. He was with her, wanting her, and she was wanting him right back, exulting in the fierce excitement he stirred, anticipation at fever-pitch, her whole body yearning for the ultimate experience of his.

'Angie…' His forehead was resting on hers, both of them gasping for breath. Her name carried a strained plea.

'Yes,' she answered, tilting her head back so he could see the unclouded need for him shining straight from her eyes.

A quick smile of relief, a sparkle of wild wicked joy. 'Is that giving me permission to undo the eight buttons that have been giving me hell all night?'

The lilting tease in his voice evoked a gurgle of laughter, erupting from her own relief and pleasure in him. 'You counted them?'

'Many times.'

He kept her lower body clamped to his, blatantly reinforcing her awareness of the desire she'd stirred, making her feel elated at her own sexual power over him as he lifted a hand to the top button, his fingers deftly releasing it from its loop.

'This one should have dissolved under the heat I subjected it to.'

The laughter welled up again.

Next button. 'Then this one should have popped open of its own accord, knowing it would get obliterated if it didn't.'

'Buttons are not sentient beings,' she said, feeling quite deliriously happy.

'But they do have two functions,' he carried on, attacking the rest. 'Opening and closing. And I didn't want you closed to me, Angie.'

Having unfastened the form-fitting bodice, his hand slid underneath it, around to the back clip of her bra, working it apart without the slightest fumble, demonstrating an expertise which might have given Angie pause for thought about that queue again, except for the swiftness of his warm palm cupping her naked breast, his fingers gently kneading its soft fullness, his thumb fanning her nipple into taut excitement, and the deep satisfaction purring through the 'Ah...' that throbbed from his throat, telling her how much he loved touching her like this.

For several moments she did nothing but revel in the way he was taking this new intimacy, the wonderful sense of his pleasure in it. Her breast seemed to swell into his hand, craving his caressing possession of it, greedy for all the exciting attention he was giving.

'Take off my shirt, Angie.' A gruff command, instantly followed by the compelling plea, 'I want to feel your touch.'

Yes pounded through her mind, though it was more a response to her own rampant desire to touch him. Her gaze swam to the row of buttons he'd left in place. Her hands lifted, eager to dispose of them, dispose of the shirt, too, bare his chest, shoulders, arms, letting her see, letting her feel the raw flood of his strong masculinity, absorbing it through her palms, skin against skin.

His breathing quickened as she glided her hands

over muscles that seemed incredibly smooth yet pulsing with a maleness which totally captivated the instinctive part of her that responded to beautiful strength in a man. And he was beautifully made. Perfect physique. It was exciting to feel the rapid rise and fall of his chest under her touch, knowing his heart had to be drumming in unison with hers.

His hand moved to her other breast, electrifying it into extreme sensitivity. 'Your jacket…get rid of it.' Hoarse need in the demand. His eyes were closed, a look of totally absorbed concentration on his face.

Exhilarated by how much he was into *feeling her,* Angie didn't hesitate, freeing herself of both jacket and bra, almost throwing herself against him as she flung her bared arms around his neck. And in the same instant he released her breast to wrap her in a crushing embrace, his mouth capturing hers, invading it with mind-blowing passion, possessing it with deep rhythmic surges, inciting a chaotic need that drove her into a frenzied response.

Waves of heat were swirling through her, crashing through her. He undid the zipper of her skirt, pushed it down over her hips—hips that wriggled their mindless consent, eager to feel closer to him. With seemingly effortless strength he lifted her out of the falling garment, scooping her off her feet and whirling her over to the bed, moving so fast Angie was still giddy from their wild kiss as he laid her down and completed the final stripping—her shoes, hose and panties—no asking permission now, just doing it with an efficient speed that screamed intense urgency, echoing the torment of coiled tension in her own body.

His eyes glittered over her, taking a searing satisfaction in her nakedness, and her heart suddenly quivered uncertainly over the rightness of what was happening here. Was it too soon? Had he cornered her into surrendering to his power? Her mind felt too shattered by raging need to think coherently.

He shed the last of his clothes, and it was as though the veneer of civilised sophistication—the gentleman image—was instantly shed, as well. He emerged from it like some primitive powerful warrior, his taut skin shimmering over muscles bristling with explosive energy, his magnificent maleness emanating a challenge that telegraphed he could and would stand up to anything, confident of battling any odds, vanquishing all opposition, winning through.

And the wolf smile was back.

Yet when he moved onto the bed, it was with the lithe prowling grace of a great jungle cat, inserting a knee between her legs, hovering over her on all fours, his head bent towards hers, his eyes blazing with the avid certainty that she was his to take as he willed...a mesmerising certainty that made every nerve in Angie's body quiver, whether in trepidation or anticipation she had no idea.

She wasn't ordinarily a submissive person. She'd always prided herself on being independent, capable of holding her own when dealing with life in general, yet she felt herself melting under the sheer dominance of this man, not wanting to fight for her own entity, yearning to merge with him, lose herself in him if that was how it was going to be.

Mine, he thought, revelling in the surge of savage triumph that energised every cell in his body, priming him to burn himself into Angie Blessing's consciousness, to put his brand on every part of her delectable femininity, use whatever means would bind her to him, take her as no man had ever taken her before.

Her eyes had a drowning look.

He felt a momentary twinge of conscience.

Dismissed it.

She'd said *yes.*

He swooped on her mouth and it said *yes,* too, her tongue as fiercely probing as his, engaging in an erotic tango that goaded him to do it now, appease the ache, fulfil the need. But that would be far too fast, not serving his purpose, and he forcefully controlled the raging temptation, tearing himself out of it, trailing hot sensuous kisses down her throat, savouring the wild gallop of her pulse-beat at the base of it.

He wanted to devour her, make her feel totally consumed by him. He moved lower, engulfing her breast with his mouth, drawing the sweet flesh deep, lashing the taut nipple with his tongue, sucking it into harder prominence, and he exulted in the convulsive arch of her body, the wild scrabble of fingers in his hair, digging, tugging, blindly urging the ravishment of her other breast. Which he did with a passion, feeding off her response, loving the vibrant taste of her, the headiest aphrodisiac he'd ever experienced.

He could hear her ragged breathing, the little moans that erupted from her throat, felt the tremors of excitement under her skin as his hand circled her stomach, his fingers threading through the tight silky curls below it, delving into the softly cushioned cleft at the apex of her thighs, caressing the slickly heated flesh, finding the most hidden places of pleasure, stroking them, feeling her inner muscles pulsing to his rhythmic touch, the hot spill of her excitement, the intense peaking of her clitoris.

He levered himself down, captured it with his mouth, moved his hands to cup her bottom, rocking her, thumbs pressing into the inner walls of the passage now yearning to welcome him. Not yet. Not yet. He drove her towards the sweet chaos of a tumultuous climax, feeling her exquisite tension spiralling higher, so high it lifted her body up to bow-string tautness.

He knew when it began to shatter, heard her cry out, exulted in her frenzied desire for him. Her hands plucked frantically at his head, his shoulders, her thighs quivering out of control, her body begging for his.

A wild energy charged through him as he surged over her, positioning them both for the entry she craved. He barely had sense enough to snatch up a condom from the bedside table and sheath himself with it before thrusting deep to settle the maelstrom of need, sharing her ecstatic satisfaction in the full penetration, feeling the ripples of her climax seizing him, squeezing, releasing, squeezing, releasing.

He held her thrashing head still and silenced her cries with a kiss meant to soothe and reassure and bring her into complete tune with him, waiting for more, wanting more, slowly tasting the promise of it, realising this was only a beginning of a sensual feast that could keep rolling on and on.

Her response was white hot at first, an almost anguished entreaty to finish it now, fast and fiercely, riding the storm of sensation he'd built to its ultimate limits, and Hugo was hard-pressed to hold on to his control, to calm her, enforcing a more conscious awareness of an intimacy that could be prolonged, that he was ruthlessly determined on prolonging so it would linger in her memory, obliterating every other memory of sexual connection she'd experienced before this.

No ghosts in this bed tonight.

Only him.

Taking absolute possession.

Angie could hardly believe Hugo was not choosing to ride the crest of her own turbulent pleasure, that he'd answered her need to feel him inside her, then stopped, as though it was enough for him to give *her* satisfaction.

Which couldn't be right.

Yet he made it feel right…the way he was kissing her…so caringly. It gave her the sense that he really treasured this gift of herself, and being so intimately joined with her was very special to him, too special not to pause over this first climactic sensation, deepening the delicious merge with a kiss that added immeasurably to how good she felt with this man.

Her inner chaos seemed to coalesce into a more intense awareness that circled around the strong core of his sexuality, anchoring her as she began to float on a warm sea of ecstasy. Her arms were strangely limp, but she managed to wrap them around him, wanting to hold all of him.

'Stay with me, Angie. Come with me,' he murmured.

The sensation of him starting to move inside her was marvellous, slowly, slowly leaving her to close tremulously behind him, retreating to the outer rim, then just as slowly pushing forward again so that her muscles clutched joyously at his re-entry, eager to have him sink as deeply as possible, wanting absolute possession of all he could give her.

He burrowed an arm under her hips, changed angles, teased, tantalised, delighted...exquisite pleasure peaking over and over again. Angie had never known anything like it...intoxicating, addictive, fantastic...her whole body keyed to feeling him, loving him, voluptuously revelling in this mind-blowing fusion.

Her legs wrapped around him, instinctively urging a faster rhythm. Her hands luxuriated in moving over him, feeling the tensile strength, wickedly wanting to test his control, make it break, draw him into the compelling overdrive that would end in his surrendering all his power to her. Somehow that was becoming more important than anything else...to take his mastery from him, make him lose himself in her, bring him to an equal place where the togetherness was truly the same.

She strained every nerve into focusing on making it happen, determined on exciting him to fever-pitch, caressing, pressing, goading with her hands, legs, kissing his shoulders, his neck, tasting him with her tongue. He laboured to catch his breath and she exulted in the tightening of his muscles, his thighs becoming rock-hard as need surged from them, forcing the more sensual rocking into a glorious primitive pounding, and she heard her own voice wildly crying *Yes...Yes...Yes...*to the beat of it.

Even more exhilarating was the animal roar that came from his throat when he finally rammed impossibly deep and spilled himself in great racking spasms, making her almost scream with the pleasure of rapturous release—her own and his, pulsating

through both of them. A passionate possessiveness
swept through Angie as he collapsed on top of her.
She cupped his face, brought his mouth to hers, and
sent her tongue deep in fierce ownership.

It seemed for a moment he was completely spent—
or surprised. It gave Angie a brief, heady taste of
being in control, seizing an initiative, but that quickly
blurred as he responded, striking sweet chords of satisfaction before ending the kiss and carrying her with
him as he rolled onto his back, tucking her head under
his chin and holding her enveloped in his embrace.

Putting himself in charge again, she thought, smiling contentedly over being Hugo Fullbright's captive.
There was no trepidation attached to it now. Her body
was still thrumming with the pleasure he'd given. Or
was it taken?

Didn't matter.

She wondered if this had just been normal sex for
him. It certainly hadn't been for her—unmatched by
anything in her previous experience. It might have
been driven by sexual attraction but it had felt as
though he was making love to her—if only physical
love—brilliant, all-consuming physical love. Far from
regretting her capitulation to it, Angie was intensely
grateful to know how it could be with the right man.

The right man...

Had she fallen in love with Hugo Fullbright?

So soon? So quickly?

Or was she simply dazed by his expertise in making her *feel* loved?

And appreciated.

And valued.

He might make all the women he chose as his companions feel like this to begin with. What happened

afterwards? How would it be tomorrow, the rest of the weekend, beyond that? For all she knew he was only intent on a *dirty weekend* with her! Though he had asked her to take a chance on him, give him time.

It was silly to start fretting over not being able to keep him in her life. That was out of her control. Hugo would undoubtedly do what he wanted to do, and whether that meant with her or without her only time would tell. Though not too much time. Not even if she loved him madly, was she going to spend three more years being dangled on the bait of a possible commitment.

If she was *right* for him...

'You're not relaxed anymore, Angie,' he said, one hand sliding into her hair, fingers seeking to read her mind. 'Tell me what you're thinking.'

She sighed away the edginess that had bitten into her contentment, then thought there was no point in not being open with him. He'd said quite plainly he didn't want her closed up. 'Just wondering how temporary I am for you.'

'Would you like not to be temporary?'

'Now there's a leading question, dodging right past mine.' She raised herself up to see if there was any hint of reservation in his eyes and was surprised to find amusement dancing at her. 'What's funny?' she demanded.

'You...thinking I might have had enough.' The wolf grin flashed out at her. 'Believe me, Angie, I'm already hungry for more of you, and if you'll excuse me while I go to the bathroom, I'll be very happy to come back and convince you of it.'

She hadn't actually been referring to sex, but he was rolling her onto the pillow next to him, extracting

himself, heading for the bathroom to get rid of the
protection he'd donned. The back view of him as he
strode away from her was just as awesome as everything else about him. *Alpha Man,* Angie thought, and
wondered why every woman in his past had failed to
hold on to him. They must have wanted to. Did *she*
have whatever it took to hold his interest beyond the
bedroom? To become a lifetime partner?

Her gaze moved to the bedside table where a heap
of condoms had spilled out of the packet he'd put
there, ready for action. He hadn't asked her if she was
on the pill, perhaps not prepared to risk her telling a
lie about that, or simply protecting himself against
any health issues. Did he always use them as a matter
of habit? Did it indicate a freewheeling sex life?

He'd certainly come amply prepared for this weekend.

But given the *Foxy Angel* angle, and her unques-
tioning acceptance of his invitation, why wouldn't he?

What would Francine have done in this situation?

Seize the chance.

Angie took a deep breath and fiercely told herself
to simply go with the flow until it didn't feel right.
She had two more days with Hugo Fullbright—two
days constantly in his company, in bed and out of it.
By the time they landed in Sydney on Monday morning, she should know if there was a real chance of
forging a relationship that would take them far beyond this weekend.

CHAPTER NINE

THE breakfast buffet in the Imperial Viking Room has to be seen to be believed,' Hugo had declared. 'And I'm *very* hungry this morning.'

So was Angie—so much energy expended last night, until sheer exhaustion had drawn them into a sleep. And again on waking up. If she wasn't in love with Hugo Fullbright, she was definitely in lust with him. He was an amazing sensualist with incredible stamina, and never in her life had Angie been made so aware of her body, which now tingled with excitement at simply a twinkling glance from this man.

Clearly he was very much into physical pleasures. Now food.

And he was right about the breakfast buffet. Hugo shepherded her around the incredible banquet laid out for people to serve themselves whatever took their fancy—every possible taste catered for: Asian, Continental, English, and all of it superbly presented to tempt appetites. Perfect fruit. Exotic pastries and croissants. Never had she seen such a wonderful selection of breakfast dishes.

'I'm going to be a pig,' Angie muttered as she kept loading a plate with irresistible goodies.

'Good! Saves me feeling guilty about indulging myself in front of you,' Hugo remarked.

She flashed him a curious look. 'Do you ever feel guilty about anything?'

He grinned. 'Rarely. Because I don't take what

isn't offered or paid for. And let me say that having you share my appetites is a joy I'd hate you to feel guilty about. Let's wallow in piggery together.'

She had to laugh.

Somehow he took any sense of sinfulness out of lusty greed, choosing to view their breakfast as an adventure into gourmet delights, encouraging her to sample far more than she would normally have done.

'Now we have to walk it off,' she told him when they finally gave up on trying anything more.

'I'll take you for a walk around the Ginza district.'

'What's there?'

'Shopping.' The blue eyes sparkled knowingly. 'The way to a woman's heart.'

It was true that most women loved shopping. And most men hated it. 'You don't have to indulge me. I'd rather we do something we'll both enjoy.'

'It's my pleasure to indulge you, Angie,' he happily assured her.

She *was* in love with him.

Absolutely drowning in beautiful feelings.

They left the Imperial Viking Room in high good humour, Angie more curious to see what the central shopping district in Tokyo offered than wanting to buy anything. She found the tour fascinating; with designer boutiques stocking clothes from all around the world, yet shops catering to distinctly Japanese culture, as well, like the one that stocked an astonishing array of umbrellas in every shade of every colour, some beautifully hand-painted or embroidered or featuring exquisite lace insertions.

'Women use them in summer to protect against the sun and heat. The streets of Tokyo are a mass of colourful umbrellas,' Hugo informed her.

'You mean like parasols?'

He nodded. 'Reduces the glare, too. Sunglasses aren't so popular here.'

'I'm not a big fan of sunglasses everywhere. Especially when people wear them indoors where there's no glare at all. It's a very irritating affectation.'

'Guarding their self-importance,' Hugo laughingly agreed.

Angie was glad he didn't seem to have any affectations, despite his VIP status. But his idea of indulging her hit a very wrong chord when he led her into a department store where the ground floor was completely taken up with displays of fabulous jewellery: gold, diamonds, pearls, every gemstone imaginable beautifully crafted into spectacular pieces.

Angie's gaze skimmed most of it in passing, recognising it was not in her affordable range, but she did stop to look at some fascinating costume jewellery, intricately worked necklaces that were exquisitely feminine and brilliantly eye-catching. They were designed like high-necked collars that sprayed out from the base of the throat, and one that was woven into a network of delicate little flowers particularly attracted Angie's eye.

It was displayed on a black plastic mould and she couldn't help touching it, thinking how wonderful it would look with her black strapless evening dress.

'Try it on,' Hugo urged, beckoning a salesgirl to help with it.

'I'm not wearing the right clothes,' Angie demurred, having donned a brown skivvy under her leopard print coat. However, she was tempted into asking how much the necklace cost in Australian currency.

The salesgirl whipped out a calculator, fingers darting over the buttons. She held it out for Angie to see the display box. Over twelve thousand dollars!

'Garnets,' the girl explained, seeing her customer's shock at the price.

'Thank you,' Angie replied, firmly shaking her head.

'Let me buy it for you,' Hugo chimed in.

Another shock which instantly gathered nasty overtones, making her query the kind of relationships he'd had throughout his long bachelorhood—mercenary women who'd jumped on him for everything? She wasn't like that and needed him to know it.

'No,' she said emphatically.

He frowned at her. 'It would be my pleasure to...'

'If you think this is the way to my heart, you couldn't be more wrong, Hugo.' A tide of scorching heat flooded into her cheeks. 'I'm not here to get what I can out of your large wallet. If that's what you're used to from other women, no wonder you don't trust what they feel for you.'

She'd gone too far.

Spoiling all the beautiful feelings between them.

Her stomach contracted in nervous apprehension as the blue eyes lost their bedroom simmer, sharpening into surgical knives that aimed at cutting through to the very heart she had steeled against *his pleasure* this time.

'What do you feel for me, Angie?' he asked very softly.

Too much. Too much, too soon, she thought, frightened to admit it when he'd just put her into the category of *bought* women. 'I was enjoying your company up until a moment ago,' she answered guardedly. 'And I'm sorry you made that offer. It puts me on a level I don't like.'

'Then please accept my apology,' he rolled straight back at her, his expression instantly changing to charming appeal. 'The offer was not meant to insult your sense of integrity. It was a selfish impulse on my part. I wanted to see you wearing the necklace. Wanted to see you taking pleasure in my gift.' His smile set her heart fluttering again. 'Will you forgive my self-indulgence?'

Confusion swirled in Angie's mind. Had she got it wrong, leaping to a false assumption about his attitude to previous relationships with women? He could certainly afford to indulge himself—the Bentley, travelling first-class everywhere, the best of everything. And she had accepted his invitation to share it all with him at no financial cost to herself.

Her pride might be leading her astray here. She wasn't used to being with a man like him. Nevertheless, she could not accept such an outrageously expensive gift on such short acquaintance, especially when that short acquaintance involved sharing his bed. It smacked of…sexual favours being paid for…and everything within her recoiled from being thought of in those terms.

'I'm sorry, too,' she said hesitantly, her hand lifting in an agitated gesture of appeasement. 'This just isn't…my scene.'

'Then let's get out of here.' He took possession of her hand and smoothly drew her into walking with him towards the exit. 'It's not far to the Sensoji

Temple—a must see in Tokyo. We could take in the east garden of the Imperial Palace, as well.'

The tension in her chest eased as he resumed his role of tour guide, coaxing her into chatting cheerfully with him, erasing the awkwardness she felt over having made such a *personal* stand about the jewellery.

Even so questions lingered in her mind.

Did he really care about the person she was...what she thought, what she felt? Or was he just a very deft womaniser, well practised at pushing the right buttons to win him the response he wanted? How much could she trust in how he seemed to be?

Hugo worked hard at recovering the ground he'd lost with Angie Blessing. Big mistake offering to buy her the necklace, putting her right offside with him. Her refusal to accept it from him had not been a ploy to make her seem different to the women he'd dated in recent years. She *was* different. No doubt about that.

And he hated the doubt he'd put in her eyes.

Hated it with a passion.

Which surprised him.

Why did he care so much about her trusting him? Certainly she'd got to him, harder and faster than he'd ever been stirred before. Last night, and again this morning, having her was more exhilarating—intoxicating—than...impossible to come up with even a near comparison. She was pure sensual magic in bed. And very, very appealing out of it.

The man who'd dumped her had to be an ego creep. Giving her up over a technician's mistake was so incredible to Hugo, it seemed only logical that the guy would be grovelling for her forgiveness come

Monday. Which meant no more false steps between now and then, opening the door for a possible reconciliation. Angie Blessing was going to be his for as long as he wanted her, and at this point in time, Hugo wasn't putting any limit on the relationship he intended to set up with her.

The temple proved a good distraction from personal issues. The huge wooden Thunder Gate and the enormous red lantern welcoming people to the temple grounds immediately caught Angie's interest. All the activity in the main hall fascinated her: people buying fortunes and good luck charms, people praying or rubbing the billowing smoke from the bronze urn on themselves for its curative powers.

They wandered down to the colourful souvenir shops and Angie happily bought three beautiful fans, hand-painted in the Japanese artistic style: a sky blue one for her mother, a dramatic black one for Francine—currently named *Hot Chocolate* on the billboard—and a very delicate pink one for herself.

'Why the pink one for you?' Hugo asked, curious about her choice.

She laughed, a self-conscious flush blooming in her cheeks, her lovely green eyes seeming to question it herself. 'I guess all girls love pink, Hugo.'

'I thought that was little girls,' he countered, thinking her answer was evasive.

'Maybe it's genetic and it never really goes away, however grown up we think we are.'

'You're not feeling grown up today?' he teased, hooking her arm around his again as they walked on, wanting her as physically aware of him as he was of her, determined on reinforcing the strong sexual connection they had.

Her lashes fluttered at him in a sidelong glance. 'You must know you make me feel very much a woman.'

He grinned at the admission. 'You make me feel very much a man.'

She sighed. 'I don't think you need any help in that department.' They were passing a shop with a display of Samurai swords and she stopped to view the display. 'In fact, that's what you should buy for yourself, Hugo.'

'What would I do with a sword?' he quizzed. 'At least you can use a fan.'

'It would be a visual symbol of what you are.'

'A Samurai warrior?'

She met his amused look with deadly serious eyes. 'I think you were born a warrior. You've learnt to put a civilised cloak over it but my instincts tell me that's your true nature.'

Her instincts were sharper than he'd realised. He'd always thought of himself as a competitor, in any arena he chose, and the will to win, or at least put in his best possible effort to win was very strong in him. 'So you see me as a fighter,' he mused, wanting to probe her thoughts further.

'A bit more than that,' she answered dryly. 'A fighter fights. A warrior sets out to conquer, determined on making his way past anything that stands between him and his goal.'

Her pinpointing of the difference lit red alert signals in Hugo's mind. How had she got this far under his skin? Most women were blinded by surface things, seeing no further than his obvious assets. Why was Angie Blessing different? What made her different? Or had he somehow revealed more of himself to her than he had to anyone else?

He swiftly decided to turn her perspective into a positive score for him. With a wry little smile, he said, 'If you think this Samurai warrior is viewing you as his Geisha girl in Japan, you're wrong, Angie.'

'I'm not here just to pleasure you?' she lightly tossed at him, but he heard the testing behind the question.

He wrinkled his brow in mock dismay. 'I thought the pleasure was mutual. Don't tell me you've felt obligated to fall in with what I want.'

'Obligated…no. Though there is a certain… expectation…attached to generosity which is all one way and I'd prefer the scales to feel more balanced.' She paused, then delivered a punch line he was not expecting at all. 'So let me buy you a sword, Hugo.'

He held up a hand of protest. 'You wouldn't let me buy you the necklace.'

'Too much on top of this trip to Japan, which I did accept.'

She was still unsettled by the idea of his *buying* her. Best to clear this issue her way right now, or it might continue to niggle, regardless of what he said. 'Hmmm…why do I sense there'll be a sword hanging over my head if I don't agree?'

'Because you're a very perceptive person?' she suggested with a grin that knew she'd won this point.

'Then let me see how perceptive you are, Angie,' he challenged, making a game of it. 'Make it your choice of sword for me.'

'Now you're putting me on my mettle,' she quipped back.

He laughed and escorted her into the souvenir shop, not really caring what she chose. If she needed some symbol of equalising the situation, let her have it. The only tension he wanted between them was that wrought by sexual desire, waiting to be satisfied.

The Samurai wore two swords—one long, the other short. Angie selected a long one which also happened to be a Japanese Navy Officer's issue sword with the Navy arsenal mark of an Anchor stamped in it. Its scabbard was black lacquered wood, very handsome. The quoted price was over two thousand dollars— more expensive than all three fans together—and it surprised Hugo that Angie didn't quibble over the price, offering her credit card without hesitation.

Was she proving she was a woman of independent means? That it was important to her to be perceived as such by him? A woman who would not be swayed even by great wealth into doing anything she didn't want to do?

He'd been presented with more expensive gifts by other women, mostly clothes they fancied seeing on him, accessories that were blatant status symbols, or *objets d'art* they thought would look good in his house. None of them had carried any real personal meaning, neither for him nor the giver.

The sword was different.

And it made him feel uncomfortable.

It was impossible to gloss over it as though it was a nothing gift, irrelevant to what was happening between them. It was a very pertinent statement, both about Angie Blessing and himself. And Hugo had the strong sense that she was pulling him into a deeper place than he'd ever been before with a woman.

As they left the shop, he couldn't stop himself from asking, 'Why a Naval Officer's sword?'

Her eyes sparkled with her own satisfaction in the choice. 'Because I can see you as a swashbuckling pirate, too, going after all the booty you can get.'

'Do I get the fair maiden, as well?' tripped straight off his tongue. She was happy with him again. It was amazing how good that felt.

She laughed, completely relaxed with him now that he'd accepted *her* gift. 'Since you've carried her off on your ship, and she's already succumbed to...' Her eyes mischievously subjected him to a once-over. '...the physical pleasures you promised...'

'And delivered?' He arched his eyebrows in a rakish query.

'Mmmh....'

The sexily satisfied hum zinged into his bloodstream, arousing strong carnal urges.

'I'd say that was a given,' she concluded, and the happy grin on her face was completely uninhibited, no shadow of any reservations about being with him.

'Let's head back to the hotel,' he said, instantly quickening their pace from a slow stroll. 'I'm feeling hungry again.'

But not for food.

CHAPTER TEN

IT HAD been an absolutely brilliant weekend, Angie thought, wishing it didn't have to end. Though, of course, time inevitably marched on and here they were in the first-class lounge at Narita Airport, waiting for their flight back to Sydney to be called. Hugo caught her smothering a yawn and shot her a rueful smile.

'Have I worn you out?'

'No. Just happy tired.' She smiled back to prove it. 'Thank you for sharing Tokyo with me, Hugo. I've loved every minute of it.'

'You made it a pleasure, Angie,' he said warmly, his bedroom blue eyes sparkling at her, making her pulse skip yet again.

But it hadn't all been about sex, she assured herself. Yesterday afternoon they had left the hotel again to take in the amazing view of the city from the Tokyo Tower's observation platform, even being able to see as far as Mount Fuji, which had been covered by snow. Then they had visited the East Garden of the Imperial Palace and drank tea in the pavilion there...until the urge for more intimacy had them hurrying back to their suite.

He was such a fantastic lover he could trigger a flood of desire just with a look. Even when they were with his Japanese hosts last night, dining at a teppan-yaki bar on the top floor of a skyscraper overlooking the city lights, eating prawns flown in from Thailand, crayfish from Sydney, and the famous Japanese Kobe steak, she was sure their appetites had been highly stimulated by the physical pleasures they had just shared, not to mention the simmering anticipation of more to come once the evening was over.

Fabulous, addictive sex.

With the deep sense of loving running all through it.

Or was she fooling herself about that? Could such feeling not be mutual? Hugo hadn't said anything. But then, neither had she. Too much, too soon?

Angie knew she wouldn't have protested if Hugo had kept her in bed all day today. Nevertheless, she was glad he'd taken her on the harbour lunch cruise, showing her more of Tokyo, spending time just talking to her, giving her the sense that he really did care about the person she was, above and beyond their wonderful compatibility in bed.

'What do you plan to do tomorrow?' he asked.

'Come back to earth with a thump, I guess. Get back to work. Face up to real life again.'

He frowned, observing her sharply from narrowed eyes. 'This weekend hasn't felt real to you?'

'It might not have been anything extraordinary to you, Hugo, but to me...' She shook her head, amazed at all they'd done together in incredible harmony. '...it's like I've been on a magic carpet ride.'

'And you expect it all to disappear in a puff of smoke?' he quizzed half-mockingly.

She hoped not. Desperately hoped not. But maybe he was referring to the *Tokyo* experience. 'I'll always have the memory,' she assured him with a grateful smile.

'No regrets?'

Her heart sank. It sounded horribly like a cut-off line. Pride forced her to say, 'None. A marvellous experience in every respect.'

'Are you saying goodbye to me, Angie?'

Shocked into realising he was misinterpreting her comments, she immediately shot out, 'Why would I want to?'

'You're not seeing me as part of your *real life*,' he whipped back, a hard, cutting edge to his voice. 'And I'm very aware I've served as a distraction from that this weekend.'

Paul…

He was referring to her acceptance of his invitation because Paul had dumped her. The weird thing was, Hugo had literally wiped her partner of three years right out of her mind and it was another shock to be reminded of him.

'Tactically, it was the best move you could have made to put yourself out of reach for a few days,' Hugo went on. 'Let him stew over his incredibly stupid and rash decision. My bet is he'll call you at work tomorrow…'

'No, he won't! Paul burnt his boats by telling—'

'Paul? Paul who?'

'Overton.' The name tripped out under Hugo's driving pressure and Angie grimaced over the absurd situation that her ex-partner should be thought of as any kind of rival by the man who had so totally superseded him.

'Paul Overton.' Hugo drawled the name as though tasting it with all the relish of a warrior given a mission that was very much to his appetite.

'He's a barrister in the public eye and the billboard blotted my copybook beyond repair as far as he is concerned,' Angie rattled out, determined on setting the record absolutely straight so Hugo understood there was no contest involved. 'I do not expect a call from him tomorrow or any time in the future. Nor do I want one. He is out of my life,' she added emphatically, her eyes flashing defiance of any disbelief on Hugo's part.

Which was ridiculous, anyway.

How could he even think she would want any other man but him after all the intimacy they had shared? Yet he was looking at her with such burning intensity, Angie felt herself flushing, as though she was somehow at fault, not giving him enough assurance that she saw a future with him. On the other hand, *he* hadn't made any firm arrangement to see her again.

Why bring up Paul now? And ask her about no regrets? It certainly hadn't *felt* like a dirty weekend, but maybe she had coloured it far too rosily with her own feelings. For all she really *knew,* Hugo might like to spend his time off work focusing on a desirable woman, enjoying saturation sex. Everything he'd said and done could have been a tactical play to win what he wanted. Was he thinking she could take up with Paul again…no harm done?

Angie's stomach started clenching.

Deciding directness was called for she asked straight out, 'Are you about to say goodbye to me?'

His face relaxed into a wolfish grin. 'No. Definitely not. I want a lot more of you, Angie Blessing. A lot more. I'm nowhere near finished with you.'

His reply should have eased her inner tension but the words he'd used and the predatory gleam in his eyes set her mind into a panicky whirl.

Finished…

It implied an end.

When he'd had enough.

As with all the other women who'd been in his life? Did he walk away and leave them behind once his appetite for them had been satisfied? She was still new to him. How long would she last?

Stop it! she fiercely berated herself.

Hugo had asked her to give a relationship with him a chance. And she would. Because it would be self-defeating not to since she felt so much *was* right with him. But she also had to learn from her mistakes, not hang on beyond what was a reasonable time for a commitment to be made. Hugo was obviously still in lust with her, but love was what she wanted, the kind of love that nothing could shake or break.

Faith in each other.

Loyalty.

Emotional security.

Her mind and heart were gripped by these needs as she heard their flight being called. Both she and Hugo rose instantly from their armchairs, action providing relief from the tension of the past few minutes. They were about to say goodbye to Tokyo but not to each other, and possibly to reinforce his intent, Hugo tucked her arm possessively around his for the walk to the boarding tunnel.

'Believe me, I'm real,' he murmured in her ear as they set off together.

She flashed him a quick smile, acutely aware of the hard muscled solidity of his claim. 'What do you plan to do tomorrow?' she asked, wanting more than his magnetic sex appeal to make her feel right with him.

'Make damned sure you don't dismiss me as a dream,' he softly growled.

Angie laughed, a wild irrepressible happiness bubbling up again, chasing away the fears of being foolishly blind to where she might be going with this man. If he was leading her down a garden path, the garden was certainly worth looking at before she closed the gate on it.

Hugo was all the more determined to keep Angie Blessing in his life now. She was a prize, definitely a top quality prize for Paul Overton to have hung on to her for three years, despite her less than sterling silver family background.

And there was such a delicious irony in the situation!

Good old Paul's overweening ego had fumbled the catch and who was there to pick up the ball? None other than the hated rival who'd pipped him at the post so many times throughout their teen years that Paul had stooped to using his parents' wealth to rip Hugo's girlfriend off him.

Not this time, Hugo vowed.

In fact, he would take great pleasure in rubbing Paul Overton's nose in the fact that Angie had moved on to him, and there'd be no buying her back. Hugo could more than match anything the Overtons had to offer by way of wealth. He had the means to shower Angie with whatever her heart desired.

Though he'd have to be careful not to overstep the mark there. She took pride in being a lady of independent means. Nevertheless, wealth was a seductive tool and Hugo intended to wield the power it gave him. He certainly wasn't about to hand any advantage to Paul Overton, who'd undoubtedly come out fighting, once he was made aware that his loss was Hugo Fullbright's gain.

But he wouldn't win, not by hook or by crook.

And how sweet it would be to see him face this defeat!

Indeed, Hugo was brimming over with exhilaration at the thought of this future confrontation as he and Angie settled themselves in the plane and they were handed glasses of champagne. He clicked Angie's in a toast, his eyes flirting outrageously with hers, promising pleasures to come.

'To Tuesday night.'

She effected an arch look, though her whole body language telegraphed yes to whatever he wanted. 'What's happening on Tuesday night?'

'I think I can manage one night without having you at my side. I'll give you tomorrow to catch up on business and sleep, but come Tuesday…dinner at my place?'

No hesitation. Big smile. 'I'd like that.'

'I'll pick you up at seven.'

'Fine.'

She happily drank to the arrangement and Hugo was satisfied nothing would change her mind. Paul Overton's pride would not allow him to call her. Not until he knew who had taken his place in her life. Which he'd discover only when Hugo chose to reveal it…with maximum impact.

A public spotlight would be perfect.

Hugo made a mental note to get James doing all the undercover work on that. With his butler network it should be no problem for him to ascertain what would be a prime meeting place and do whatever was required for Hugo and Angie to be present, parading their relationship.

Of course, by the time that was put into action, it would be too late for Paul to make a recovery.

Hugo was ruthlessly determined on ensuring it was too late.

Far too late.

He was not about to give up this woman.

Not to anyone!

CHAPTER ELEVEN

As THE Bentley crossed the Harbour Bridge, taking her home from the airport, Angie swivelled around in her seat to look out the back window and check the billboard. Amazing to think only a few days had passed since it had caused such a change in her life!

The photo of Francine—*Hot Chocolate*—was still on it, as it should be since her friend had paid for a full week's advertising. It was only Monday morning. Three full days of exposure so far, four more to go. Angie wondered if it had brought in any real possibilities for the outcome Francine wanted.

Hugo's gaze followed the line of hers. 'Your business partner,' he said, recalling what she'd told him.

'Yes. Francine Morgan.'

'Does *Hot Chocolate* really describe her?'

Angie grimaced. 'Probably *Foxy Angel* is more true to Francine's character but she couldn't use that after the mistake was made of putting my face with it instead of hers. I think, in her angst over the situation, she just went for something madly provocative.'

'Stirring the pot.'

'I just hope it doesn't backfire on her, landing her in big trouble. Francine is my best friend as well as the marketing force in our design company. We share the apartment, too.' Angie checked her watch. They had landed at six-thirty, but being first-class passengers, there'd been virtually no delay in the arrival

112

procedures at the airport. It was only seven-thirty now. 'She'll still be at home.'

'Then I'll get to meet her.' Spoken with warm anticipation.

Angie glanced sharply at him, remembering he'd admired her friend's enterprising nature, though he'd attributed it to herself at the time. 'Francine may want to steal you from me,' she said wryly.

He laughed and squeezed her hand. 'No chance.'

Her heart tap-danced in pleasure, yet to Angie's mind, in the marriage market he was a prize that any woman would covet. Even fight over. 'You must know you're a very attractive package, Hugo.'

His eyes instantly lost their twinkle of amusement and acquired the searing intensity of twin blue lasers. 'I'm very much taken by you, Angie. Don't doubt that for a minute.'

It was good to hear.

Nevertheless, the plain truth was they'd basically spent an exclusive weekend together, no intrusion from their normal social circles, and most of the time dominated by the strong sexual chemistry between them. Angie couldn't help wondering how their relationship would fare, given the various pressures of their day to day lives, not to mention the judgements of people who were close to them.

She looked at the chauffeur in the driver's seat. James had greeted them cheerfully at the airport, welcoming them home. He appeared to have his attention completely focused on the road, but he was probably listening intently to whatever was going on in the back seat. He gave no indication of it, not by so much as the tiniest snort, but he had to be fitting her into the context of Hugo's previous women, making comparisons.

Would he favour her or work against her if he saw the relationship turning serious? He might not care to have any woman interfering with his running of Hugo's household. Why hadn't Hugo married before this?

He's been waiting for me, Angie told herself in a determined burst of positive thinking. It was what she wanted to believe, and when they arrived at her apartment and Hugo escorted her inside, briefly making the acquaintance of Francine before taking his leave, his manner definitely reflected that she—Angie Blessing—held prime position in his heart.

'Wow! What a sexy hunk! Those eyes…and he's obviously smitten with you, Angie,' was Francine's comment the moment Hugo had gone. 'No need to ask how the weekend went. I bet he's dynamite in bed.'

'It wasn't just sex,' Angie protested, flushing at the inference that nothing else mattered.

'Got to have the spark to start with,' came the knowing retort. 'And Hugo Fullbright is sparking on all cylinders! It's clear to me that you two are up and running, Angie. And good for you, I say! Even better for me.' She rolled her eyes in relief. 'Takes away my guilt over Paul. Who, I might add, has made no contact though he must have seen that *my* photo has gone up on the billboard, proving what we told him was true.'

'The truth was irrelevant,' Angie said dryly, drawing up the handles of her bags, ready to roll the luggage into her bedroom. 'Come and tell me how *Hot Chocolate* fared while I unpack.'

'Brilliant! I'm snowed under with responses,' Francine declared, pirouetting with glee as she danced ahead to open Angie's bedroom door for her. 'I've got bug eyes from reading them through on the computer this weekend.'

Angie shot her a look of concern. 'I thought the name you used might draw some gross stuff.'

Francine waved an airy hand. 'I've eliminated all those.' Her eyes twinkled with happy anticipation. 'Kept only the clever ones. And don't you worry. I'm vetting them very carefully. If they don't come up to my exacting standards...no meeting.'

'What precisely are your exacting standards?'

She grinned. 'Someone who works hard at winning me.'

Angie cocked a challenging eyebrow. 'There doesn't have to be a spark?'

'Oh that, too. Naturally I'm asking for photographs. After all, they have seen mine.'

'You think you can tell from a photograph?'

As Angie heaved her larger bag onto the bed, ready to unpack, Francine bounced around to the other side, wagging a confident finger. 'The eyes have it,' she asserted. 'Your Hugo has just demonstrated that. I look for sparkly, intelligent, wicked eyes.'

'Wicked?'

'Definitely wicked.'

'That might not be husband material,' Angie warned, once again reminded that Hugo was a long-time bachelor, though he had certainly gone all-out to win her. But what if winning was an end in itself?

'Well, at least I should have a lot of fun finding out,' Francine declared, totally undeterred from her mission for marriage.

Fun…or heartbreak?

Angie shook off the doubt.

Tomorrow night she'd be with Hugo again. Nothing was going to stop her—or Francine—from pursuing what seemed right for them.

Hugo focused his mind on what had to be done as James drove him home to Beauty Point on Middle Harbour. 'I want you to acquire two tickets for all the upcoming ballet performances, James,' he said, having decided that was top priority.

'Ballet, sir?' The astounded tone was comment enough on Hugo's previous lack of interest in that artistic area.

'It's never too late to try something new.' Especially with Angie, Hugo thought.

'Of course not, sir. One's experience can always be broadened.'

'Exactly. Have you seen a ballet, James?'

'Oh yes, sir. Never miss a performance. It's always quite splendid. I'm delighted to hear Miss Blessing enjoys it, too.'

Hugo noted the warm approval in his voice—definitely a recognition of top quality. No doubt this would facilitate James' co-operation in securing what was required.

'In fact, sir, I have prime seats already booked for the ballet season. No problem to give them to you for the…uh…duration.'

'Very kind, James, but the duration could be longer than such self-sacrifice could stand. See if you can book more.'

'As you wish, sir,' came the cheerful response.

Apparently the idea of a *long* relationship met his

approval, too. Hugo wondered how Angie had scored so many positive points in his butler's book. While James had invariably acted with faultless courtesy towards the women Hugo had brought home in the past, he usually remained extremely circumspect in any remarks about the relationships. Still, there was no time to reflect on this change right now. Instructions had to be given.

'When you unpack, you'll find a Samurai sword in my bag. I'll leave it to your good taste to find the best way of displaying it in my bedroom. Some place it can't be missed, James.'

'A sword, sir?' he repeated in some bemusement.

'A gift from Miss Blessing.'

'I will see that it's *prominently* displayed, sir.'

'Before tomorrow night.'

'Do I understand Miss Blessing will be...uh... joining you tomorrow night, sir?'

'I thought dinner on the patio. I trust you can organise something special, James. For eight o'clock?'

'Any dislikes I should know of, sir?'

'Only seaweed soup.'

'Ah! Splendid to have so much leeway in preparing culinary masterpieces. Fussy eaters are very restricting.'

'Please feel free to be as creative as you like,' Hugo drawled, amused by his butler's enthusiasm.

A sigh of pleasure. 'At last! A lady who will appreciate my training with gourmet food.'

'Let's not lose perspective here, James. I have always appreciated your skill in the kitchen.'

'Thank you, sir. I didn't mean to imply...'

'Fine! I also want flowers sent to Miss Blessing's

office today. Let her know I'm thinking of her. What do you suggest? She likes pink.'

'Then it has to be carnations and roses, sir. And lots of baby's breath for contrast.'

'Baby's breath?' Hugo wasn't sure he liked the sound of that.

'Tiny white flowers, sir. Very feminine.'

James sounded so smugly satisfied with the idea, Hugo let it go, telling himself the exotic Singapore orchids had certainly served their purpose. 'Okay. Get it done. The note should read...*Until tomorrow.*'

'That's all, sir?'

'It's enough, James. Sorry if that blights your romantic soul.'

'As you say, sir, best not to go overboard. Less can sometimes be...'

'When I want your advice on how to deal with a woman, I'll ask for it,' Hugo cut in dryly. 'In the meantime, I have another task for you. Do you know about the Overton family?'

'Old establishment posh people, Wallace and Winifred Overton?' was instantly rattled out. 'Son, Paul, heading for a Blue Ribbon seat in the Liberal Party?'

'The same. I want you to find out what parties or social events they'll be attending in the next month or so. Very discreetly, James. I'd prefer not to have them know I'm interested in meeting them.'

'With a view to business, sir?' Clearly his curiosity was piqued by this uncharacteristic interest in *posh people.*

Hugo was not inclined to explain. This was personal. Deeply personal. 'Just report back to me as soon as you can. Anything to do with politics won't suit, but a fashionable ball or a premiere…'

'A social occasion that you might naturally attend,' James swiftly interpreted.

'Exactly.'

'And I should wangle you an invitation to it?'

'Two invitations. I shall be escorting Miss Blessing.'

'Does Miss Blessing have an interest in the Overton family, sir?'

Hugo grimaced at the linkage James had uncannily seized upon. 'No, she hasn't,' he said emphatically, though, in fact, Hugo felt a compelling need to have that proven. It wasn't just winning over Paul. He wanted to be certain there was no rebound effect running through Angie's attachment to himself. 'Nor do I want this mentioned to her,' he added. Surprise gave no room for pretence.

'Miss Blessing will simply be accompanying you,' James smoothly interpreted.

'I want her at my side…yes!' he answered curtly, finding himself somewhat discomfited by these questions.

Was he sure he wanted to do this?

Paul Overton wasn't part of his life anymore, hadn't been for twenty years. Though he had been a motivating force behind the desire to make big money, to build up so much wealth that winning or losing no longer depended on what could be given. It came down to the man.

Who was the better man for Angie Blessing?

Because it was Paul she'd been with for the past three years…Paul who had dumped her, not the other way around…Hugo wanted him to fight to get her back. Fight and lose.

Then he would know beyond any shadow of a doubt that Angie was his.

Not by default.

Her choice.

Regardless of what Paul offered her.

And he'd offer her all he could because it was Hugo who'd taken her over and that could not be tolerated by Paul Overton.

What it came down to was Hugo wanted closure on that old battleground. And he especially wanted closure because Angie Blessing was involved.

The confrontation had to take place.

CHAPTER TWELVE

DINNER on the patio was going brilliantly. The balmy summer evening made being outdoors particularly pleasant and James congratulated himself on perfect stage management.

Of course, the location itself—overlooking the very creatively landscaped swimming pool right above Middle Harbour, plus the clear starlit sky—had its natural beauty, but the addition of strategically placed candles with subtle floral scents added to the romance of it all, and his table setting with the centrepiece of miniature pink roses was pure artistry.

Miss Blessing had obligingly worn pink, as James had anticipated she would after yesterday's gift of flowers—subliminal choice—and his boss was wearing the white clothes which had been laid out for him. They looked a very handsome couple. A fitting couple.

James found himself humming the wedding march as he worked away in the kitchen, loading the silver tray with the sweets course. Highly premature, he told himself, but all his instincts *were* picking up promising signs.

The weekend in Tokyo had clearly inspired desires that were far from quenched. One could say they were burning at furnace heat out there on the patio. And never before had James received such meticulous and far from the usual instructions about the continuation of an affair.

Ballet!

And not just flowers to be sent. Exotic Asian flowers last Thursday. *Pink* flowers on Monday. When had his boss ever taken note of a woman's favourite colour?

Then there was the Overton family element that also had to be connected to this new relationship. What could his boss possibly want from self-styled upper class snobs? Normally he'd avoid them like the plague. Total contempt for their values. Surely the only reason he would go out of his way to meet them was for the sake of Miss Blessing.

Whose photo, apparently, should not have been on that billboard. This circumstance certainly added to the fascinating scenario. James had actually thought it was rather a dodgy self-marketing stratagem, coming from a lady who shone with natural class. Nice to know his judgement had not been astray. On the other hand, there was no doubt that Miss Blessing did have a flair for taking bold initiatives…giving his boss a Samurai sword.

That cut to the quick.

Clever woman.

Yes, it could very well be that his boss had met his match.

James carried the tray out to the patio, benevolently observing the glow of contentment his dinner had raised, not to mention the holding of hands across the table and two faces happily absorbed in drinking in the sight of each other.

'My pièce de résistance,' he announced. 'Orange almond gateau with drunken apricots swimming in Cointreau. King Island cream on the side.'

'Oh! How blissfully sinful!' cried the lady, her

lovely green eyes lit with delight at this special of-fering.

James barely stopped himself from preening over his gourmet masterpiece. He did so enjoy having his talent appreciated. 'A pleasure to serve you, Miss Blessing,' he crooned.

'I've never had such a wonderful meal!'

'Thank you.' James swiftly passed on the credit to get the flow of appreciation moving in the right di-rection. 'Mr. Fullbright did request something extra special for you. Without seaweed.'

She laughed and squeezed the hand holding hers. James felt an emanation of hungry urgency coming from his boss that had nothing whatsoever to do with food.

'You have quite outdone yourself, James,' he said, smoothly adding, 'Just leave this with us now. I think we'll forgo coffee in favour of finishing the wine.'

Rampant desire barely held in check.

Clearly aphrodisiacs were not needed. However, no harm in having replenishment on hand. A dish of the Belgian chocolate truffles he'd purchased to serve with the coffee could be put on the bedside table.

'Very well, sir.' He clicked his heels and bowed stiffly from the hips. 'May I wish you both a very good night.'

He loved doing that stuff. It was so deliciously camp under the guise of proper formality. Though he was tempted to swagger a little as he made his exit, as his acute sense of hearing picked up Miss Blessing's whispered words.

'Your butler, chauffeur—whatever he is to you—is worth his weight in gold, Hugo.'

'Mmh…that's just about what he costs, too,' came the dry reply.

Worthy of my hire, James thought, sailing out to his kitchen with all the majestic aplomb of the Queen Mary 2. He'd laid the scene. It was up to his boss now to capitalise on it. And there had better not be just sex on the menu, because Miss Blessing—bless her marriageable heart!—had the stars of love in her eyes. Anyone could see that.

As Angie savoured the glorious taste of the sweets course, she felt as intoxicated as the drunken apricots. Though not from alcohol. She couldn't help thinking this was the kind of courtship dreams were made of— being magnificently wined and dined in an exclusive romantic setting, everything arranged for her pleasure. Life with Hugo had felt so extraordinary during the weekend in Tokyo. She hadn't really expected that sense of awe to continue, but here she was feeling unbelievably privileged again.

She loved his beautiful home. She loved everything about the man sitting opposite her. She even loved his butler. Best of all was the mounting evidence that Hugo was certainly not viewing this relationship lightly.

When the masses of pink roses and carnations had been delivered to the office yesterday, even Francine had commented, 'What we have here are serious flowers, Angie. You've definitely got him hooked.'

Angie had shaken her head. *Hooked* was the wrong word. Hugo Fullbright would never let himself be caught. He was the hunter, the jungle cat, the wolf, the warrior. If he took a partner, it was for his pleasure. The big question was, would she be a lasting pleasure?

The hope she was nursing had certainly received a big boost tonight with Hugo's announcement that he had acquired tickets for them for the rest of the ballet season. This had to mean he planned on their being together for months, at the very least. And he cared enough about *her* pleasure to open his mind to sharing her interest.

It wasn't just lust on his part. It couldn't be. Besides, she had to concede those feelings were mutual. The sizzling desire in his eyes had her body buzzing with excitement, and there was no denying she loved his touch. Simply holding hands was enough to set her mind racing towards—wanting— more intimate contact.

Having consumed most of the delicious gateau, Angie set down her spoon, smiling ruefully at Hugo. 'I'm so full I can't eat any more. Will James be terribly offended if I don't finish it?'

'No.' The vivid blue eyes glinted wickedly. 'He'll probably think I raced you off to bed before you could.'

'Is that what you usually do?' tripped off her tongue, instantly raising a tension she didn't want between them.

Making comparisons to previous relationships was an odious intrusion when she should simply be revelling in being the sole focus of his attention. Yet once the challenge was out, she realised the answer was important to her.

Did Hugo have seduction down to a fine art?

Was the aim to dazzle her into compliance with whatever he wanted?

He'd sat back in his chair, the sexual magnetism suddenly switched off as he looked at her with the weighing stillness of every sense alert, sifting through what was coming at him. Angie's pulse skipped into a panicky beat. The warm harmony she had been revelling in was gone, supplanted by this tense stand-off. Had she spoiled their evening together?

'Yes, it is what I usually do,' he stunned her by saying, his eyes locking onto hers with searing intensity. 'I won't deny I have a strong sex drive and I've never been involved with women who don't want to go to bed with me. On an evening such as this, the natural follow-up would be to seek and enjoy more physical pleasures. Do you find that wrong, Angie?'

'No.' It was reasonable. Perfectly reasonable. And she felt stupid and flustered by his logic. 'I just…wondered…'

'How special you are to me?' he finished softly.

Heat flooded up her throat and scorched her cheeks, but she bit the bullet and stated the truth as she saw it. 'I still feel I'm on your magic carpet ride. All this…' Her hands moved in an agitated gesture to encompass the luxuries he could and did provide. 'You could overwhelm any woman if you set your mind to it. And I do feel overwhelmed by the way you're treating me, but I don't know what's in your heart, Hugo.'

'My heart…' An ironic little smile tilted his mouth, softening the hard look of a keenly watchful predator, weighing up the most effective way to pounce.

It gave Angie's own heart a jolt when he surged to his feet, swiftly stepping around the table to seize her hands and draw her up from her chair.

'Feel it,' he commanded, pressing her open palm to the vibrant heat of his chest.

Her whole body seemed to be drumming at his closeness—the forceful contact, the compelling intensity of his eyes blazing into hers. Was she feeling his response to her or hers to him? Angie didn't know, was helpless to discern anything beyond the physical chaos he stirred in her.

'You hold it,' he fiercely declared. 'You're pounding through my bloodstream. I ache for you. I can't take another second of separation.'

His mouth swooped on hers, passionately plundering, obliterating all Angie's concerns with the sheer excitement that instantly coursed through her. A melting relief soothed her jagged nerve-ends as Hugo swept her into a crushing embrace. She wanted this. Needed it. Loved the feverish possessiveness of his hands renewing his knowledge of her every curve, fingers winding through her hair, holding her in bondage to him.

Hungry kisses.

Greedy kisses.

And the desire for more and more of him erupted like the hot lava of a volcano, a force of nature that was unstoppable.

'Come with me.' Gruff urgency.

He broke away, grabbed her hand, pulled her along with him.

Angie's legs seemed to float in the wake of his stride, weak and wobbly yet caught up in the flow of energy driving him. She was too dazed to question where he was taking her. He tugged. She followed. Strong purposeful fingers encompassed hers, transmitting a ruthlessly determined togetherness, no separation, feet marching to a place of his choosing. Into the house. The luxurious living room facing onto the patio was a blur. Down a wide corridor.

A bedroom.

It had to be his.

And he'd raced her there.

Her dizzy mind registered a strikingly minimalist room, just the bed dominating a huge space—a king-size bed with many pillows—and lamp tables on either side, a soft glow of light from them. The top bed-sheet was turned down, ready...*ready*...and there was a silver dish of chocolates...*seductive* chocolates...

'Look!'

The command meant nothing to her. She *was* looking, feeling a terrible jumble of emotions, telling herself that the *readiness* didn't matter. Whatever had gone on in this bedroom in the past didn't matter. Only what she and Hugo felt together mattered. Yet if it was no more than elemental chemistry...

'Not there!' Terse impatience.

He spun her around to face the wall opposite the bed. A huge plasma television screen was mounted on it, and below that a long, low chest storing what seemed like massive amounts of home theatre equipment. Obviously he could lie in bed and...

'You see?'

His pointing finger forced her gaze upwards, above the mind-blowing size of the television screen.

The Samurai sword!

Angie's heart kicked with a burst of wild exultation.

Hugo had not set her gift aside as a meaningless souvenir. He had been so impressed—so pleased—by her choice, the sword was now hung in a prime place for his private pleasure, mounted on brass brackets that made it a fixture, not something that could easily be moved, on or off display as it suited him.

'It's the last thing I see at night and the first thing I see in the morning,' he said, stepping behind her and wrapping his arms around her waist, drawing her back against him. He lowered his head beside hers, purring into her ear. 'It's like having you speak to me, Angie. Does that tell you how special you are?'

'Yes.' The word spilled from a gush of a delight in the wonderful knowledge that she had touched him deeply. This was not a superficial attraction. Not for her. Not for him.

His hands slid up and cupped her breasts and the pleasure of his touch swelled through her on a blissful wave of happiness. She leaned back into the powerful cradle of his thighs, wanting to feel his arousal, wanting him to know it felt right for her.

He grazed soft kisses over the one bared shoulder of the silky top she wore—a warm, sensuous, tasting that made her quiver with anticipation. 'I want to make love to you, Angie,' he murmured. 'I want to sink myself so far into you that we're indivisible. I want...'

'Yes...yes...' she cried, not needing to hear any more, wanting what he wanted.

But he did not race into it.

'Don't move,' he growled. 'Let me show you how special you are. Look at the sword, Angie. Look at it...and feel how I feel about you.'

She looked at it, stared at it, remembering what she'd said about him being a warrior, determined on getting past anything that stood in his way...and he slowly removed her clothes, caressing them from her flesh, his hands sliding, stroking, palms gently rubbing her nipples into pleasure-tortured peaks, fingers finding the moist heat he'd excited, using it to drive her awareness of her own sexuality even higher. And his mouth trailed kisses everywhere, a hot suction that was incredibly erotic, a gentle licking that was intensely sensual.

The sword…an anchor engraved on its handle.

Was Hugo the man who would anchor her life?

Always be there for her?

She had the sense of being completely taken over by him, territory he was marking as his own, and she stood there, so enthralled by what he was doing to her that passively letting it happen didn't seem wrong. She didn't know if he was taking or giving. Somehow that was irrelevant. She felt…*loved*.

And when he finally moved her onto the bed, a mass of tremulous need crying out for him, the image of the sword was still swimming in her mind, and as the strong thrust of him slid deeply inside her, she saw herself as made to receive him, a perfect fit, like the black lacquered scabbard encasing the steel of the man, holding the heart of the warrior.

True or not…it was what Angie felt.

No memory of Paul Overton flitted through her consciousness.

And the women in Hugo's past…no substance to them. None at all.

The only reality was *their* union.

CHAPTER THIRTEEN

WOULD she spend the coming weekend with him?

Angie's mind was still dancing with *yes* to that question—*yes, yes, yes* to anything at all with Hugo—as she raced into her apartment to get ready for work the next morning. Francine accosted her before she reached her bedroom, taking in her bright eyes and flushed cheeks, not to mention the happy grin.

'So...Take Two went off with flying colours,' she concluded.

'And Take Three is already on the drawing board,' Angie literally sang.

'Well, I've had some luck, too,' Francine drawled smugly, stopping Angie in her tracks.

She looked expectantly at her friend, hoping that somehow *Hot Chocolate* had produced some magic for her.

'You'll never guess.' Francine laughed, shaking her head as though even she thought it was a miracle. 'I got an e-mail last night from the boy next door.'

'What boy next door?' There were no eligible guys in this block of apartments.

'From the old days. When we were kids in our home town before I moved to Sydney. Tim did an engineering course at Newcastle so our lives kind of diverged and we lost track of each other.'

'He saw your photo on the billboard?'

'Uh-huh. Then wrote to ask if it was me. Gave me his e-mail address in case it was. We've been chatting on the Net half the night, catching up and feeling out where we are now.'

'So where is he?'

Francine grinned. '*Not* married. And we're meeting for lunch today.'

'For the spark test?'

It had been Francine's prime requisite for starting a relationship, yet she wasn't dressed in her sexy *out there* best. She was wearing a yellow linen shift dress, more classy than sexy, though the colour did stand out enough to say *look at me,* stating a confidence in herself which Francine never lacked.

'You know, I haven't even thought about that,' she replied in a bemused tone. 'I like Tim. Always did. We were buddies in our teens though…' She grimaced. '…he never asked me out or anything. Never asked any girl out. He always had part-time jobs to help out with his family. Big family. Not much money.'

'Then you're just looking to renew a friendship?' That didn't exactly jell with this degree of pleasure.

She shrugged. 'Who knows? Tim was always a bit of an enigma. Most of the kids considered him a nerdy type but he wasn't really. He was just too smart for his own good. It's not popular, having stand-out brains, always questioning how things work. But you could have a really good conversation with him, not just slick boy-girl talk.' She heaved a happy sigh. 'I'm *so* looking forward to having that kind of company again.'

Without the strain of always trying to sell her attributes, Angie thought. Which answered the question of why Francine wasn't doing her power-play. However, she was in such a good mood, Angie hoped the meeting would work out well for her. With *a spark* happening, as well. Francine deserved a really good guy, one who truly appreciated the person she was. Though it was still a worry that the billboard photograph was the means of reforging this contact.

'This Tim...what's his full name?' Angie asked, a warning on the tip of her tongue.

'Tim Haley.' Francine rolled out the name as though it tasted like a sweet, heady wine.

Angie instantly checked herself from possibly striking a sour note. It had been a long time since their teens. *Hot Chocolate* might have provoked some sexual fantasy Tim Haley was now pursuing, taking the advantage of previous acquaintance. However, if this was so, Francine would find out soon enough.

Angie smiled. 'Reminds me of Halley's Comet. Zooming into your life out of the blue. I wish you all the best with him.'

Francine laughed. 'Thanks, Angie. At least I know he genuinely likes me.'

Genuine liking...

Yes, it was all important in a lasting relationship, and Angie thought about that on and off all morning as she worked beside Francine in their Glebe Road office. The materials they'd priced for the Pyrmont apartment block had to be ordered, contractors lined up to do the painting and tiling. It was difficult to focus her mind on the job when it kept returning to what she had with Hugo.

Strong sexual attraction was such a powerful distraction to really knowing how deeply the liking went. In that respect, an old-fashioned courtship was probably a much better proving ground. Would Hugo have pursued an involvement with her if she hadn't gone with him to Tokyo?

Impossible to ever know that now.

She had plunged headlong into this relationship and now she had to cope with having moved way out of her comfort zone.

So far there was nothing not to like about Hugo and she was fairly sure he thought the same of her. They enjoyed each other's company…just talking together. Though how much was he actually listening to her? Weren't his eyes always simmering with what he wanted to *do* with her?

Making love…

Angie had no doubt about the physical loving.

Apart from that, she did have the certainty that she'd touched something in Hugo's heart with the gift of the Samurai sword. He was also willing to take her to the ballet. Both of which proved he listened to what she said. Cared about what she said.

And their work sort of dovetailed, with Hugo being the driving force behind building new places and her colour co-ordination expertise making them even more attractive. This provided a common interest, making them compatible on more than one level.

It was probably foolish, worrying about sex being a dominant factor in their relationship. If the spark wasn't there, nothing would have happened between them. In fact, she'd be wallowing in depression from being so summarily dumped by Paul, hating him, hating herself for ever having thought she loved a man who could wipe her off for something she hadn't even done.

Three years…

How long did it take to really *know* a person?

Maybe never.

The thought slid into Angie's mind... *We colour them in how we want them to be.*

Yet instincts played a part, too, she quickly amended. Her instincts had been questioning Paul's *rightness* for her before last Thursday, and they were definitely signalling a great deal of *rightness* with Hugo.

All the same, after Francine left for her lunch date with Tim Haley, Angie found herself on tenterhooks, waiting to hear the outcome of their meeting, wanting to know if 'the spark' meant more than liking. The two didn't necessarily go hand in hand and her friend could be in for big disillusionment if Tim came onto her hard.

It was a very long lunch. When Francine finally returned to the office, she walked in as though floating on Cloud Nine, the dreamy smile on her face telegraphing that friendship had definitely turned into something else.

'Well?' Angie prompted impatiently.

The dreamy smile turned into a sparkling grin. 'I think I've found the man I'm going to marry. And what's more, I think he's got the same idea in mind.'

'From one meeting?' It seemed too incredible.

She laughed in a giddy fashion. 'Even I can hardly believe it.' She threw up her hands in a helplessly airy gesture. 'There I was, explaining about the billboard, trying to find a marriageable guy because I just wasn't meeting anyone I fancied as a possible husband, and Tim asked straight out if I could I see him in the frame.'

'And could you?'

Francine nodded as she hitched herself onto

Angie's desk to confide all to her. 'I was hoping he
might be interested if I toned myself down a bit. Not
hit him full on. But it was he who knocked me out.'

'Big improvement on the past?'

'Just…a lot more impact. Grown up. Filled out.
And the way he looked at me…'

'Wicked?' Angie quickly slid in, since *intelligence*
was not in question.

Again Francine laughed, her own eyes twinkling
with happy anticipation. 'Lurking behind warm and
cosy, I think. Waiting for the green light.'

'Did you give it to him?'

'Not straight up green but certainly a very encouraging amber.'

'You're truly attracted to him?'

'I sure am!' came the delighted reply. 'It turns out
that he patented an invention of his in the U.S. and
made pots of money from it, and he's so confident
now…'

'So he can well afford a wife and family,' Angie
said, mentally ticking off Francine's requirements.

'No problem.'

'Then why amber? Why not green?' Angie queried,
not understanding why Francine hadn't seized her
chance.

'I didn't want Tim to think I was considering him
for marriage out of sheer desperation. Like I'd grab
him just because he was putting himself on the line.
He's special. And I want to feel special to him.'

Yes.

Hugo had made her feel very special last night.

And he was special, too. Incredibly special.

'Besides…' A determined look settled on
Francine's bright face. '…I still want my husband to

win me. Show me I'm truly *the one* for him. Convince me of it.'

Angie nodded. 'Passion,' she murmured, her heart lightening with the certainty of Hugo's passion for her.

'Deep and abiding,' Francine said with considerable passion herself, making Angie realise how very serious her friend was about Tim Haley.

'He did give you reason to believe he might have serious intentions and wanted to pursue them with you?' she pressed worriedly.

'No question.' She lightened up, bubbling with excitement again. 'I tell you, Angie, I was so flabbergasted, I had to keep on testing if he was real or not. He said, like me, he's ready for marriage and wants to have a family. When he saw my photo on the billboard he started remembering what a good connection we'd had as kids, and our chatting last night, and again today, demonstrated a level of easy communication he'd never had the pleasure of with any other woman. Tim thought that was an extremely good basis for marriage.'

'Smart man,' Angie couldn't help commenting.

'I told you he was smart.' Francine grinned. 'And I do love smart.'

Hugo was smart, too, picking up on her needs, answering them, but had the thought of marriage even vaguely crossed his mind? Did she answer *his* needs?

'I've invited Tim to dinner with us tomorrow night.'

'Us?'

Francine slanted her a wise look. 'I can control what happens in our own home. You can be the chap-

erone, Angie. Make it proper and respectable. I want
Tim to court me.'

Courting…not plunging into an intimacy that overwhelmed every other consideration. In fact, Angie
realised she wasn't in control of anything with Hugo.
He just kept sweeping her away…

'If he's truly serious, it won't put him off,'
Francine ran on. 'Besides, I don't want him to think
I'm after his money and what it can buy. If he comes
to our place, it won't cost him anything, and the apartment will show him I've done well for myself, too.'

Angie frowned…shades of Tokyo with Hugo prepared to buy her the necklace. That had been bad.
Bad, bad, bad.

'You're sure this marriage frame is not just a ploy
to pull you in?' she asked, worrying if they were both
giving their trust to men who were on different paths
to the one she and Francine wanted them to take.

'Tim wouldn't do that to me.' With a very direct
look that burned with conviction, Francine added, 'I
know him, Angie. Long-time knowing. People don't
change their character. I think his success in business
has given him the confidence to go after what he
wants and he figures the timing is now right for us.'

Long-time knowing.

Angie wished she had that with Hugo. Though it
hadn't served her well with Paul, had it? Three years
to find out what came first with him. Though that
wasn't entirely true. She had known Paul always
came first for Paul. She just hadn't wanted to see how
little *she* meant to him.

It was different with Hugo. Completely different,
she fiercely told herself.

Francine hugged herself exultantly as she waltzed

from Angie's desk over to her own, then flopped into her chair, arms opening out to encompass a whole new world. 'Just think! Last Thursday, life was the absolute pits! Six days later and our prospects are looking bright! You've got Hugo and I've got Tim. Happy days ahead!'

It sounded good.

It was good.

Angie vowed to give up negative thinking right now. Just because she hadn't known Hugo very long didn't mean she couldn't be blissfully happy with him. As she had been last night. And this morning. And was sure to be next weekend, too. They were on a journey together. There was no solid reason to think this journey wouldn't have a happy end.

CHAPTER FOURTEEN

THE State Governor's black tie dinner and charity auction…

Angie eyed her reflection in the full length mirror on the door of her clothes cupboard…hair up in an elegant style, make-up as good as she could do it, around her neck the gold pendant necklace on which hung a pseudo emerald—costume jewellery she'd bought to go with the black strapless evening dress, earrings to match—and the dress itself, so perfect for her it had been impossible to find anything better.

The only problem was she'd worn it before.

With Paul.

Which made it feel…somewhat tainted…with memories she didn't want.

And Paul was bound to be at *this* function. Angie had known it the moment Hugo had mentioned he'd bought a swag of tickets for it, saying it was a very worthy cause, raising money for a new children's hospital. At a thousand dollars a ticket, he'd put out a lot of money, booking a table for ten, inviting his closest business associates and their wives along, Francine and Tim included especially for Angie, making a party of it.

Hugo's obvious pleasure in his plan, and the expense already incurred, had made it impossible for her to say she didn't want to go. If she'd tried to explain it was because of Paul, it would have been like a negation of what she felt with Hugo. He might have thought she still cared about Paul Overton and she didn't.

The truth was, she just didn't want a night with Hugo spoiled by any show of Paul's contempt for her. The brutal call he'd made to dump her demonstrated an attitude he would undoubtedly carry through in public. Pride alone would demand it of him.

His parents, friends and associates would be there, as well, all of whom probably regarded her as something of a tart because of the billboard photo. And Paul wouldn't have told them the truth about that. Oh no! It would have messed up *his* story of what had happened.

Maybe she should tell Hugo…warn him there might be some unpleasantness. But if he then thought she still cared about Paul…

No!

Best that she try to shut the whole horrible business out of her mind. Concentrate on Hugo and how great their relationship still was, even more intimate after three months of being together in most of their free time from work. She would not let Paul's presence spoil anything, not even her pleasure in this dress. It looked great on her. In fact, this was as good as she could look…for Hugo.

'Anything wrong, sir?' James asked.

Hugo instantly smoothed out the frown James had observed in the rear-vision mirror. 'No. Where are we?' he asked, glancing out the side window of the Bentley.

'Almost at Miss Blessing's apartment. Five minutes away. We're on time.'

'Good!'

Angie was always ready on time, another thing he liked about her. He hated being kept waiting. Only at their very first meeting... and that was because of the shock of seeing her photo on the billboard instead of Francine's, probably worry about Paul Overton's reaction to it, too.

'The State Governor's dinner... I did get it right, sir? Meeting your requirements?' James asked a trifle anxiously.

'Perfectly,' Hugo assured him. 'Thank you, James.'

No way could he not go through with it now. He hadn't liked Angie's reaction to attending the special charity function... going all quiet, probably realising instantly it was the kind of event the Overtons would attend. She shouldn't have cared. With him at her side, she should have been happy with the opportunity to defy whatever they thought.

The hell of it was, he still felt uneasy about it.

He would win over any machinations Paul Overton came up with to take Angie away from him tonight.

Of course he would win.

That wasn't the point anymore. The problem was... Hugo suspected he'd made a bad move where Angie was concerned and he didn't know why it was bad. Tonight should be a triumph for her. Why wasn't she feeling that? Given everything they'd shared over the past three months, nothing the Overtons could do should touch her.

The Bentley came to a halt. Hugo picked up the jewellery box, determined on getting Angie to wear his gift. He hoped it would make her feel better about appearing at his side tonight, lift her spirits, give her joy.

'Good luck, sir,' James tossed at him as he alighted from the car.

Hugo didn't answer.

Luck had nothing to do with tonight.

If he was the right man for Angie, nothing should touch what they had together.

The doorbell rang.

Angie grabbed her evening bag, took a deep breath, told herself she had nothing to worry about, and went to open the door to the man she truly did love with all her heart. He looked breathtakingly handsome in his formal black dinner suit and his smile instantly sent a rush of warmth through her.

'Is Francine gone?' he asked.

'Yes. Tim picked her up half an hour ago. He wanted to take her somewhere else first.'

'May I come in for a minute?'

She nodded, slightly mystified by the request. Though his eyes sent their ever-exciting message of wanting to make love with her, a minute wasn't long enough and they were all dressed up and ready to go. Nevertheless, once inside with the door closed, he took her hand and drew her into her bedroom with such an air of purpose, her stomach started to quiver.

'Hugo…' she began to protest, then fell silent, mystified even further by the box he set on the bed.

'Face the mirror,' he commanded, moving her to do so and positioning himself behind her. His hands lifted to the catch of her necklace. 'This looks lovely on you, Angie,' he purred, 'but I want to see you wearing something else.'

He whipped the pendant away, opened the box, and Angie was stunned to see him lifting out the necklace she had admired in Tokyo. 'You bought it?' she gasped as he hung the exquisite collar of garnet flowers around her neck.

'Over the telephone when we got back to the hotel.' He flashed his wolf grin. 'While you were in the bathroom. I arranged for it to be delivered to the reception desk for me to collect before we left.'

'I told you not to.'

'You bought me the sword, Angie.'

'But…' She touched the fabulous piece of jewellery, loving it, yet feeling confused about Hugo's motives.

'No buts. I've kept it for you until now so you can't have any doubt about its being a true gift, without any strings attached. There's no reason for you not to accept it,' he stated unequivocally, making it a churlish act to even quibble about it.

Angie sighed, surrendering to his forcefulness, telling herself this was solid proof of how much Hugo cared about her, buying this gift and holding on to it until he felt the timing was right. 'Thank you. It's beautiful,' she whispered, choked up by a flood of mixed emotions. A ring on her finger was what she really wanted from him. To hide her inner turmoil she busied herself taking off the pseudo emerald earrings. 'I can't wear these with it.'

'Put these on.' He held out a matching set for the necklace, long tiers of the exquisite garnet flowers, almost like miniature chandeliers, probably costing as much as the necklace.

Her fingers fumbled over putting them on. At last they were fastened in her lobes and the effect with the accompanying elaborate collar was mesmerising...dramatic, exotic, an abundance of richness that dazzled the eye.

'You look magnificent,' Hugo declared, his eyes burning possessively at her reflection in the mirror.

Angie found her voice with difficulty, but the image facing her demanded she ask the question. 'Is this why you wanted to take me to a formal function? An occasion fit for the gift?'

Something savage flickered in his eyes. 'The gift is worthy of you,' he growled, then bent his head and kissed her bare shoulder, hotly, as though he wanted to brand her as his. But a necklace, however magnificent, didn't do that, Angie thought. Only a ring did. And the ring didn't have to be anywhere near as extravagant as this gift.

'Now we can go,' Hugo murmured, meeting her gaze in the mirror again with a look of searing satisfaction.

Angie nodded and smiled, though she wasn't smiling inside. She felt distressingly tense as Hugo tucked her arm around his to escort her out to the Bentley.

James was standing to attention by the open passenger door, waiting to see them seated. He flashed Angie an appreciative once-over. 'May I say you look splendid, Miss Blessing!' Warm approval and admiration were beamed at her.

'Thanks to Hugo,' tripped off her tongue, touching the necklace nervously as the thought slid through her mind that the fabulous showpiece jewellery had turned her into an ornament on his arm tonight.

It was not a happy thought.

Shades of being with Paul.

Angie fiercely told herself Hugo wasn't Paul. He was nothing like Paul. And she was not going to let her experience with Paul Overton twist up her feelings for Hugo.

The boss has made a big mistake with that lavish jewellery, James thought, covertly observing his passengers as he drove them towards Government House. The lady was not impressed with it. She kept touching it as though it was an uncomfortable cross to bear, not a glorious pleasure to wear.

She wasn't like the other women who'd traipsed through his boss's life. Couldn't he see that? He was going to stuff up this relationship if he didn't realise he had real gold in his hands. And James was nursing quite a few doubts about the purpose of this charity function that the Overton family would be attending.

A few subtle questions in the right places had elicited the information that Angie Blessing had been Paul Overton's partner for three years, the relationship breaking up just before the billboard incident. So what was the boss up to? Proving he was the better man? Loading the lady with flamboyant jewellery to show that she was his?

This was not a good scenario.

James had bad vibes about it.

Very bad.

As he drove into the grounds of the Governor's official residence, he hoped his boss was right on his toes tonight, because James figured some very fancy footwork would be needed to come out of this situation the winner.

Angie had been to Government House before. With Paul. Tonight it was to be drinks on the terrace first, then dinner and the charity auction in the function room. As James drove the Bentley into the grounds, she saw a string quartet playing on the terrace overlooking the gardens and a good smattering of people already there, enjoying the ambience of the evening. She wished there was a crowd. The jewellery she was wearing was so highly noticeable, she would have felt less on show in a crowd.

But, of course, they were arriving at the stated time on the tickets. Hugo had no patience with unpunctuality. He considered being fashionably late an affectation that was plain bad manners.

There would inevitably *be* a crowd, Angie assured herself. This was definitely a top A-list function. Everyone who was anyone would come, some to be seen, others to prove how wealthy they were, movers and shakers.

It was a relief to see Francine and Tim strolling up from the gardens. Angie needed her friend's support tonight. Not even the secure warmth of Hugo's hand holding hers could settle her nerves.

Francine spotted the Bentley and waved. The flamboyant red car undoubtedly stood out like a beacon in the cavalcade of black limousines arriving. Red...garnets...did Hugo want her to stand out, too? Showing her off...*his* woman? She had to stop thinking like this. It wasn't fair. It wasn't right.

There were ushers lined up to open car doors, saving the time it would take a chauffeur to do it. The moment James brought the Bentley to a halt, the back door was opened and Hugo was out, helping Angie to emerge beside him, tucking her arm around his again. *Curtain up,* she thought, and hated herself for thinking it. There was nothing wrong with Hugo feeling proud of her. She should be glad he was.

Francine and Tim were waiting for them on the edge of the terrace. Angie noted her friend was glowing with happy excitement, almost jiggling with it beside Tim who wore the air of a man enjoying sweet success.

Francine's sparkling eyes rounded in astonishment at seeing the spectacular jewellery that had replaced Angie's far more modest choice. 'Wow!' she breathed, her gaze darting to Hugo and back to Angie with a raising of eyebrows.

Angie nodded, acutely conscious of the elaborate earrings swinging back and forth.

'That's some gift, Hugo,' Francine said in an awed tone.

'Angie carries it off beautifully,' he purred with pride.

'That she does,' Tim agreed, grinning away, his confidence in himself and Francine's attachment to him not the least bit dented by Hugo's extravagant giving.

He thrust out his hand in manly greeting and Hugo had to detach himself from Angie to take it. Francine skipped around Tim and thrust out her hand for Angie to see. 'Look! Look!' she cried, positively bubbling with excitement.

A diamond ring!

A beautiful big sparkling solitaire firmly planted on the third finger of her left hand!

An engagement ring—marriage proposed and agreed upon!

A stab of envy sliced through Angie so fast, shame drove her into babbling every congratulatory expression she could think of, hugging Francine, hugging Tim, forcing herself to be happy for them because she was. She truly was. Especially for Francine who had finally found the kind of husband she'd wanted. And the love shining from both of them left no doubt about how they viewed their future together. Absolute commitment.

For them this was a night to remember.

For Angie…her friend's happy situation underlined her darkest thoughts about tonight.

She wasn't Hugo's bride to be.

The jewellery he'd placed around her neck made her feel like a high-priced tart.

She wanted to feel good about it.

But she didn't.

Couldn't.

It felt the same as it had in Tokyo…the kind of thing Hugo habitually did for his women. It didn't mark her as anyone special to him. It said she was just another one in a queue who would eventually pass out of his life. Regardless of the three months they'd been together, nothing had really changed for him.

Though maybe she was wrong.

Angie fiercely hoped she was.

CHAPTER FIFTEEN

As soon as the Master of Ceremonies requested guests move into Government House, ready for dinner which would soon be served, Hugo wasted no time leading his party inside to the function room. They were ushered to their table and he designated the seating, ensuring for himself a clear view of the people streaming in for the business end of the charity evening. Angie, of course, was placed beside him.

He had not spotted the Overtons in the crowd outside and he had not tried searching for them. The mood of his own group of guests had been very convivial, celebrating the happy news of Francine's and Tim's engagement, and he'd wanted to keep it that way, especially since he'd sensed Angie's tension easing as bright repartee flowed back and forth, evoking merry laughter.

Besides, he felt no urge to hurry the confrontation he'd wanted. In fact, he was in two minds whether to push it or not. Mostly he wanted Angie to feel happy with him, happy to be at *his* side.

Waiters served champagne. Appreciative comments were made about the table settings, the floral decorations, the chairs being dressed in pastel blue and pink covers, a reminder that this function was to benefit children. Hugo kept a watchful eye on the people being ushered to their tables.

He saw Paul's parents come in with a relatively senior party, their haughty demeanour instantly striking old memories of them looking down on his parents as not worth knowing, and being vexed with him whenever he snatched some glory from their son. Though they had deigned to congratulate him. With thinned lips.

It occurred to Hugo that Paul had been born to live up to their expectations, bred to an arrogant belief that he should be the winner. But that didn't excuse some of the tactics he'd used to be the winner. The self-styled noble Overtons did not have nobility in their hearts. They simply had a mean view of others.

Angie didn't notice them. She was busily chatting to his guests, being a charming hostess, very good at drawing people out about themselves. Which was another thing he liked about her, not so full of herself that she always had to be the focus of attention. She even took an interest in James' life, not treating him as just a super servant on the sidelines. No meanness in her heart.

How the hell had she been fooled by Paul into staying with him for three years?

That really niggled at Hugo.

Especially since Paul had dumped her, not the other way around. As it should have been. How could she not have seen, during all that time, what an egomaniac he was?

At least she knew it now.

But something about Paul Overton still affected her and Hugo needed to know what it was.

Focusing all her attention on the company at the table and forcing herself to make bright conversation had served to lift Angie's spirits. She was determined on making this a fun night for Francine, setting her own inner angst aside. They were all here to enjoy themselves and she was not going to be a spoilsport.

The champagne helped.

Though she almost choked on it when Francine, who was sitting beside her, leaned over and whispered, 'Paul has just come in.'

Angie swallowed hard and flicked her friend a derisive look. 'I'm not interested.'

'Neither you should be,' Francine fervently agreed. 'But I've got to say the woman on his arm isn't a patch on you, Angie. Big come down.'

'His choice,' Angie answered flippantly.

'And Hugo leaves him for dead.'

In every way, Angie fervently confirmed to herself. It didn't matter that he hadn't yet offered her an engagement ring. The jewellery was a special gift, bought months ago to please her when the time was right. Hugo went out of his way to please her, which surely meant she was special to him. She just wished this gift had been presented to her on some other occasion.

She smiled at Francine, then directed a question at Tim, not wanting to even look at Paul. Though Francine's comment about his new woman piqued her curiosity enough to take a quick glance towards the entrance to the function room.

Recognition was instant—Stephanie Barton, daughter of one of the leading lights in the Liberal Party, one of the best political connections Paul could make. Well, the grass certainly wasn't growing under Paul's ambition, she thought cynically, and her set course of ignoring him was suddenly made much easier.

His view of her was totally irrelevant. In fact, he

could look at her with as much contempt as he liked. He was the one who deserved contempt, trading himself for political advantage.

Hugo watched Paul scan the room, budding politician in action. He was not paying any attention to the woman hanging on to his arm. Not a beautiful woman like Angie. Not even a pretty woman, although she had certainly worked hard on effecting a stylish appearance. Hugo decided she had to be a well-connected woman—silver spoon matching up to silver spoon.

As Paul's gaze roved around, picking out notable people, nodding and smiling when he received some acknowledgment, Hugo rather relished the shock that would hit him when he caught sight of his old rival. It had been a long time, but the animosity on Paul's side would undoubtedly still be there. On his own side? Only the problem with Angie's feelings weighed heavily. That had to be resolved.

The moment of recognition came.

A visible jolt and double take, his mouth thinning in displeasure as he visually locked horns with Hugo, silently challenging the effrontery of *his* presence in a place where he didn't belong. Except money was the only requisite here, and his contemptuous grimace revealed he knew Hugo was now loaded with it.

The contempt did it.

Irresistible impulse took over.

Hugo leaned back in his chair and stretched his own arm around the back of Angie's chair, deliberately drawing Paul's attention to her, ramming home how big a loser he was, despite the silver spoon cramping his mouth. Angie should have been treated

as a queen, which was what she was—so far above
other women she was right off the scale. And for Paul
to have dumped her...well, let him at least acknowl-
edge her worth now!

The moment he saw Angie, his whole face tightened up. He stared, then jerked his head forward, jaw
clenched with determination not to look again. At either of them. Especially the two of them together.

His party was ushered to a nearby table and since
all the tables were round, he could and did manoeuvre
the placings so that he sat with his back turned to
Hugo and Angie—an act of disdain, but Hugo wasn't
fooled by it. Paul didn't want to face what he'd just
seen. He had no weapons to fight it.

Unless Angie gave him an opening.

Hugo swiftly tuned in on what was happening at
his table. Tim was explaining one of his inventions
to the rest of the party and Angie was turned to him
in listening mode. She seemed more relaxed now and
Hugo relaxed himself, reasoning that if Angie had
been disturbed at the thought of meeting Paul again,
she would have kept a watchful eye out for his arrival
herself, and clearly she hadn't.

Or was determined not to.

In which case, there was still a problem.

The dinner served was of the finest, most expensive
foods, all beautifully presented and accompanied by
a selection of wines chosen to complement each
course. Francine raved about everything but Angie
found it difficult to eat. She was still too conscious
of the elaborate collar around her neck. It felt as
though it was choking her.

A children's choir came in to entertain with traditional Australian songs, starting with *Waltzing Matilda* and finishing with a rousing rendition of *I Still Call Australia Home*. Angie turned around in her chair to face and applaud them. She caught sight of Paul's mother staring at her from the table closest to the stage. Or rather staring at the jewellery Angie was wearing. Then her gaze flicked up and she raised her nose in a sniff of dismissal before looking away.

Fine! Angie thought savagely. I didn't want you as a mother-in-law, anyway!

Yet she found her gaze skimming around the tables for Paul and found Stephanie Barton seated almost parallel with her on the other side of the room. The man next to her faced away from where Angie was but it was Paul all right. Had he seen her and deliberately chosen to keep his back turned to her?

That was fine, too, Angie decided.

Ignoring each other was the best way through this function.

But the garnet collar felt tighter than ever.

It was a relief when the sweets course was taken away and the auction started. Tim bid for and eventually won a walk-on part in a movie which was about to be shot in Sydney.

'I didn't know you wanted to be in movies,' Francine quizzed when he was triumphant.

'It's for you,' he answered, grinning from ear to ear. 'I couldn't afford to take you to the movies when we were kids. Now I'm going to have the pleasure of seeing you in one.'

They all laughed and Angie thought how nice Tim was, and how lucky Francine was to feel free and happy about accepting any expensive gift from him.

He wasn't buying her. He loved her. And the proof of that was on Francine's finger.

Coffee and petit fours were served as the auction continued at a wild pace, an amazing variety of goodies up for grabs. Huge interest was stirred amongst the men when Steve Waugh's autographed bat was offered. The recently retired cricket captain had been named 'Australian of The Year' and had reached the status of legendary hero amongst the sport's fans.

The bidding for the personal bat was fast and furious. Hugo joined in. Angie couldn't help noticing Paul did, too. Hugo's jump bid to ten thousand dollars seemed to be the clincher for him, but as the auctioneer wound up the sale, Paul suddenly called, 'Fifteen,' opening it up again.

'Twenty,' Hugo called, without so much as blinking an eyelid.

A hushed silence as everyone waited for a possible counter-bid. Paul didn't look around to see who had beaten him. He faced the auctioneer and raised his hand, drawing the attention of the whole room to himself as he called, 'Thirty,' in a terse, determined voice.

The auctioneer raised his eyebrows at Hugo, 'Do we have a contest, sir?' he asked, clearly wanting to whip one up. 'It's for a very good cause and this bat hit a century for Steve Waugh.'

'Then a century it is,' Hugo drawled. 'I bid one hundred thousand dollars.'

It evoked a huge burst of applause.

When it finally died down, the auctioneer gestured to Paul and whimsically asked, 'A double century, sir?'

Paul forced a laugh and waved the offer away, conceding defeat.

'That's very generous of you, Hugo,' Angie said warmly, impressed that he had contributed so much for a children's hospital.

He swung around to her, his eyes glittering with the savage satisfaction of a warrior who has swept all before him, his mouth curling with a deep primeval pleasure in his victory. 'To the children, the spoils of war,' he said.

'War?' Angie didn't understand.

'Cricket might be a sport but it's also a battle. A fight to the finish,' he explained.

'Well, you sure hit that other bidder right out of the playing field,' Tim said appreciatively.

'What you might call a deep six,' Hugo agreed with his wolf grin.

The other men at the table chimed in with good-humoured comments involving cricket terms which clearly amused them. Not ever having been a cricket fan, the repartee was completely lost on Angie. Francine, as well, who suggested they slip off to the ladies' powder room.

'Paul was livid at losing,' Francine whispered as soon as they were out of earshot of their party. 'I bet he was deliberately bidding against Hugo because of you.'

Angie glanced at Paul's table before she could stop herself. Stephanie Barton was staring venomously at her and even as their eyes caught, she said something to Paul, and from the nasty twist of her mouth Angie assumed it was some jealous snipe. Paul, however did not look around and Angie quickly turned her own gaze away.

'More likely he wanted to make a charitable

splash,' she muttered to Francine. 'He'd be angry at being frustrated, having decided what to bid on.'

'Well, I'm glad he's not having a happy night,' Francine shot back with smug satisfaction. 'Serves him right for being such a stupid snob as to dump you because...'

'That's water under the bridge,' Angie sliced in.

'True. And Hugo is much more giving.' She heaved a happy sigh. 'I do love generous men.'

Generous, yes, but what of the motive behind the generosity?

Angie didn't voice that thought. It touched too closely on the current ache in her heart—an ache that grew heavier as she refreshed her make-up in the powder room and the ornate jewellery from Japan mocked her dream of a forever love with Hugo.

Self-indulgence...that was what he'd called his impulse to buy it for her in the first place. He was still indulging himself with her. He'd wanted the pleasure of seeing her wear his gift and she'd let him have his way. He'd won her compliance. Won it all along. And maybe winning was what it was all about with him. Like with Steve Waugh's bat—decide on something—get it!

Interesting question...what was he going to do with the cricket bat, now that he had it? Angie resolved to ask him when she returned to their table. However, she and Francine were no sooner out of the powder room, than they were waylaid by a furiously determined Paul Overton.

'I want a word with you, Angie. A private word.' He grabbed her arm. 'Out on the terrace.'

'Let go of me,' she cried, angered at his arrogant presumption. 'I have nothing to say to you, Paul.'

'Well, I have a hell of a lot to say to you,' he seethed, the hand on her arm a steel clamp as he started pulling her away with him.

'If you don't let Angie go, I'll get her guy to come,' Francine threatened. 'You don't want a scene, Paul,' she added sarcastically.

'By all means get Fullbright,' Paul snarled at her, carelessly revealing knowledge of his name. 'While I tell Angie the truth about my old school buddy.'

'What?' Shock weakened Angie's resistance to Paul's dragging her outside with him. Her feet automatically moved to keep up with him.

'You're just a pawn in his game,' he shot at her, his eyes glittering with the need to shoot more than her down. He dropped a scathing look at the necklace as he jeered, 'Dressing you up like a queen to checkmate me.'

'You have nothing to do with us,' she protested, though a host of frightening doubts were clanging through her brain.

'I have *everything* to do with him parading you here tonight,' Paul grated out viciously.

Was that true?

They were outside, away from everyone else. The auction was still continuing in the function room— the auction that had provided a battle between Hugo and Paul, with Hugo bidding an enormous sum…to be charitable or to thwart a rival?

It had been a gorgeous Indian summer day but the night air was crisp now, bringing goose bumps to Angie's skin. Or was it the chill of a truth she didn't want to believe? She told herself Paul was an egomaniac and he was reading the situation wrongly, hating being publicly beaten, taking his anger out on her.

'This is absurd!' she insisted. 'Hugo was interested in me before he ever knew I'd had a relationship with you.'

'Sure about that?' Paul whipped back at her.

'Yes, I am,' she retorted heatedly.

'How soon did he learn about me?'

The quick insidious question stirred more emotional turbulence. She'd given Paul's name to Hugo at Narita Airport, at the end of their *dirty weekend*. But he'd bought the jewellery before that, on the Saturday, she reasoned feverishly, so he'd meant to continue their affair. Hugo's interest in her could not hinge on Paul.

'It doesn't matter,' she muttered, firmly shaking her head.

'You think it's not relevant?' Paul mocked. 'When you told him about me, did he mention we knew each other?'

No, he hadn't. Not a word. 'School was a long time ago, Paul,' she argued, not wanting to concede any substance to the point being made.

'Some things you don't forget.'

'Like what?' she demanded.

He told her.

About the intense rivalry between them.

About the chip on Hugo's shoulder because he hadn't been born to a life of privilege.

About the girl who'd dumped Hugo for Paul.

He fired bullets at her so fast, Angie was reeling from the impact of them. She could see the influence they might have had in forming Hugo's ambition, motivations...and they hammered home the point...*some things you don't forget.*

But there was one big flaw in Paul's scenario and she leapt on it. 'But *you* dumped *me*. Why would Hugo want your discard?' she flung at him.

'Good question.'

The drawled words startled them both into swinging around.

Hugo strolled forward to join them. He appeared completely relaxed, supremely confident, yet Angie sensed the powerhouse of energy coiled within, ready to be unleashed. It played havoc with her nerves which were already torn to shreds under Paul's very personal attack on her position in Hugo's life. She didn't want to be a bone of contention between them, yet all her instincts quivered with the sense that it was true. Terribly true.

It was a dangerous smile Hugo bestowed on Paul, and the airy gesture he made as he closed in on them had a mesmerising sleight-of-hand about it. 'The answer is...I want Angie because she is beautiful...inside and out. Nothing at all to do with you, Paul. Though I do wonder that you were such a fool as to let her go.'

Paul's jaw clenched. Sheer hatred burned in his eyes. 'Not such a fool that I didn't finally see she was no more than a cheap whore who'd sell herself to the highest bidder,' he bit out in icy contempt.

Angie gasped at the painful insult, her hand instantly lifting to her throat, wishing she could tear off the damning necklace.

'You're welcome to her, Fullbright,' Paul jeered.

'Always the sore loser,' Hugo mocked silkily. 'Do choose your weapons more carefully. You wouldn't want that vote-winning smile rearranged.'

Paul's shoulders stiffened, bristling with the aggression stirred. 'I didn't lose anything worth having,' he snapped.

'No? Then why drag Angie out here? Why do your venomous best to destroy her trust in my feelings for her?'

'Feelings?' He snorted derisively. 'I was doing Angie a favour, letting her know she'd been used by you.'

'How benevolent! Strange how I never noticed that trait in your character. Much more in keeping that you'd badmouth me so I'd lose, too.'

'You kept her in the dark, Fullbright. That speaks for itself.'

'Or does it say you were simply not a relevant factor?'

'Angie's not stupid. She can put it together.'

'I'm sure she can…from the way you treated her.'

'Still got your debating skills, I see.'

'Sharp as ever.'

'But not sharp enough to pass the real test, Fullbright.' A glint of triumph accompanied this challenge.

Angie had been sidelined as a spectator to the contest being waged, but suddenly she found herself the target of Paul's *test*. 'If you hadn't cheapened yourself on a public billboard, I would have married you, Angie,' he threw at her. 'If you think Fullbright's *feelings* for you will lead to marriage, think again. He'll never take you as his wife and you know why?'

She stared at him, feeling all the vicious vibes being aimed at both of them.

'Because I had you first,' he flung down, then

swung on his heel and strode off with the arrogant air of having finished with people who were beneath him.

Which left Angie and Hugo alone together—an undeniable statement hanging between them.

She had given herself to Paul first.

CHAPTER SIXTEEN

SOILED goods...

It was an old-fashioned phrase, out of step with life as it was lived now, yet it slid into Angie's mind and set up camp there, burning into her soul.

'Are you okay, Angie?' Hugo asked, his laser blue eyes probing hers for possible problems.

She looked blankly at him, feeling herself moving a long distance away from this whole situation, detaching herself from the entangled relationships with Hugo and Paul, standing alone. Chillingly alone.

'You can't believe I'd be influenced by what Paul is,' he said in a tone of disgust. 'But if you need to talk about it...'

'No!' The word exploded from her need to be done with the mess she had been drawn into. 'I want...' *to finish this right here and now.* Yet wouldn't Paul feel some filthy triumph if she left the scene before the night was over? Not only that, her disappearance would worry Francine, cast a shadow on her friend's happy night. She lifted her chin with a heightened sense of holding herself together and said very crisply, 'I want to return to our table. We've been missing too long already.'

'Fine! Let's go then.'

He clearly interpreted her reply as a positive decision towards him, smiling his relief and pleasure in it as he offered his arm. She took it, merely as a prop to present the right picture so Francine would be

pleased that she had sent Hugo to the rescue. And
Paul would not have the satisfaction of knowing how
deeply she had been hurt.

Oddly enough, the physical link to Hugo had lost
all its sexual power. There was ice in her veins, not
one trickle of heat getting through from the contact
with him. She hated being a trophy woman. Once this
evening was over and they were in the privacy of the
Bentley, she would stop being one, and never, never
again fall into that horribly demeaning trap.

Hugo was delighted that Angie was dismissing the
confrontation with Paul as not worth any further consideration. Sour grapes on Paul's part. Which, of
course, it was. Clearly her mind was satisfied that her
former lover did not impinge on their relationship in
any way whatsoever and she was well rid of him.

Closure had definitely been effected.

Though as they reentered Government House,
Hugo noted Angie's cheeks were flushed and she was
holding her head so high it smacked of proud defiance, which told him she had been stung by Paul's
personal insults to her. Perhaps badly stung. And his
previous doubts about whether he was making the
right moves came crashing back.

What had he achieved tonight?

Yes, it had felt good to outbid Paul in the auction,
though that wasn't particularly important to him. He'd
meant to bid for something anyway, giving to a charity that would benefit children.

And it had felt good, seeing Paul's reaction to finding Angie attached to him now.

Being the winner always felt good.

But at what cost if Angie was hurt by it?

Out there on the terrace, he had felt savagely satisfied that Paul's behaviour had stripped any wool from Angie's eyes where her ex-lover was concerned, but now he had the strong and highly disturbing sense that it had not righted the wrong he'd been feeling.

Far from it!

Paul's last childish shot of the night—*I had her first*—started some deep soul-searching which Hugo pursued relentlessly while he played out the charade of continuing a bright happy party at his table.

Had he been driven to arrange this encounter because he needed affirmation from Angie that she truly felt he was the better man? Right from the beginning he'd felt possessive of her. Finding out she'd been with Paul for three years...and it hadn't been *her* decision to break the relationship...had definitely struck him hard.

Not the sexual aspect of it. That didn't matter a damn. After their first night together in Tokyo, he'd had no doubt he and Angie were so sexually attuned to each other, the kind of physical intimacy they shared was something uniquely special to them. That had never been a problem.

It was the long attachment to Paul that had niggled.

Would she have married him if the billboard mistake hadn't happened?

Hugo's gut twisted at that thought.

But she knew better now, he told himself. Tonight Paul had surely obliterated any lingering sense of being robbed of a good future with him. She couldn't possibly regret losing him now. He'd demonstrated beyond any doubt what a mean-spirited bastard he was.

All the same, Hugo was acutely conscious that

Angie was not turning to him with a renewed flow of positive feeling. She was focusing almost exclusively on the others at the table, barely acknowledging his contributions to the conversation, not touching him and not welcoming any touch from him, actually detaching herself from contact with him. Not obviously. Under the guise of turning her attention to someone else or making a gesture that seemed perfectly natural.

It made Hugo increasingly tense. He craved action, a resolution to whatever was distancing Angie from him. As the auction drew to a close, he took out his mobile phone and sent a text message to James, ordering the car up, ready for a quick departure. He suffered through the wind-up speech by the M.C., applauded the end of it, then rose from his chair, thanking his guests for their company, wishing Francine and Tim well again, and taking his leave of them, ruefully announcing his work schedule demanded an early night.

Angie was quickly on her feet without any assistance from him, but she did submit to having her arm placed around his for the walk out of the function room. Again she held her head high and despite the many admiring and envious glances she drew as they made their exit, her gaze remained steadfastly forward, acknowledging nothing.

The Bentley was waiting.

James sprang to attention the moment he saw them, opening the passenger door with his usual flourish. 'Did you have a good evening, sir?' he asked as Angie stepped into the car and settled on the far side of the back seat.

Hugo handed him the cricket bat. 'Belonged to Steve Waugh. Take care of it, will you, James?'

'A prize, indeed, sir,' James enthused.

Not the one he most wanted, Hugo thought darkly
as he moved in beside Angie who sat with her hands
firmly in her lap, her gaze averted from him, not the
slightest bend in her towards the intimacy they had
so recently shared.

Hugo waited until the Bentley was on its way out
of the Royal Botanic Gardens before he broke what
he felt was highly negative silence. 'I'm sorry about
what happened with Paul tonight,' he started gently,
hoping she would unburden the hurt she felt so he
could deal with it.

'Are you, Hugo?' she answered in a flat, disinter-
ested tone.

He frowned, sensing one hell of a chasm had
opened up between them.

Then she turned her head and looked directly at
him, her green eyes as cold as a winter ocean. 'You
planned it. Please don't insult my intelligence by denying it. You planned how this evening would play
out.'

'No. Not how it did,' he quickly corrected her.

'You knew Paul would be there, just as I knew he'd
be there,' she said with certainty.

'You could have said something if you didn't want
to risk a social meeting with him,' he countered.

A mocking eyebrow was raised. 'Avoiding him
would have given him an importance he no longer
had to me.'

'Sure about that, Angie? I sensed you didn't want
to see him and I readily confess I didn't like the feeling that…'

'It was bound to be unpleasant if we met,' she cut
in crisply. 'That was my only concern. But you must

have known that, Hugo. With your old history with Paul, you must have known he'd force a meeting…and you deliberately led me into it.'

The accusation sat very uncomfortably. Hugo didn't have a ready reply to it.

'But *I* didn't matter, did I?' she continued. 'It was between you and him. I was just the means to…'

'No!' he asserted vehemently. 'You do matter. Very much. And I'm deeply sorry Paul subjected you to…'

'The truth?'

'I doubt Paul Overton has spoken the truth in his whole damned life! As for *his* version of my history with him, I'm sure that was twisted to suit the purpose of undermining what we have together.'

His aggressive outburst didn't stir one ripple in her icy composure. She simply sat looking at him, apparently weighing the strength of what he'd claimed. Then very quietly she asked, 'What do we have, Hugo?'

'You know what we have,' he shot back at her. 'A great rapport. We enjoy each other's company. Every time we're together it's good.'

Her mouth twisted in bitter irony. 'Good enough to think of marrying me?'

Marriage!

Hugo shook his head in furious frustration at how poisonous Paul's barbs had been.

'Well, at least you're honest about that,' Angie commented wryly, misinterpreting his reaction.

'For God's sake, Angie!' he protested. 'I needed to get your hangover from Paul out of the way first.'

'*My* hangover!'

She didn't believe him. The scorn in her eyes

goaded him into saying, 'We've only been together
three months. Let's be reasonable here. You were
content to be with Paul for three years without getting
a proposal from him.'

Big mistake.

Huge mistake!

Incredibly stupid to compare the two relationships!

Her face instantly closed up on him and she sat
facing forward again. Her hands lifted and one by
one, removed the earrings from her lobes, dropping
them onto her lap.

'What are you doing?' he demanded in exasperation at her apparent choice not to argue with him.

No answer.

It was all too obvious what she was doing.

She removed the necklace, too, then gathered the
jewellery together and placed it on the seat space between them. 'I don't want this, Hugo. I did tell you
not to buy it,' she flatly stated.

'It suited you. It looked great on you,' he asserted,
feeling a totally uncharacteristic welling of panic at
this clear-cut indication she was cutting him off.
'There's no reason for you not to keep it,' he insisted
heatedly.

She flicked him a derisive look. 'It makes me feel
like a high-priced whore.'

Paul again!

'You know you're not one, Angie!' he threw at her
furiously.

'Yes. I know,' she said dully, her head turning towards the side window, away from him.

'Then why are you letting Paul Overton colour my
gift to you?'

'He didn't. I felt it when you put it on me tonight,

Hugo,' she answered, speaking to the night outside, the darkness seeping into her mind, shutting him out.

'You gave me the Samurai sword,' he fiercely argued. 'Why can't I give you a gift without you thinking...'

'The sword wasn't for public show,' she cut in wearily.

How could he make her understand? He had wanted her to wear his gift tonight to show how much *he* valued the woman Paul had rejected, to make her feel like a queen compared to other women. For her to know that this was how he thought, and feel it, especially when she saw Paul again.

'I would have broken up with Paul if he hadn't leapt in first,' she said, and slowly, slowly, turned her gaze back to his. 'You see, I finally realised I was a trophy woman to him, not someone he really loved for who I am...the person inside. I guess I was dazzled by other things about him but I did finally see...' Her mouth twisted. '...and I have no intention of spending the next three years being your trophy woman, Hugo.'

'That's not what you are to me,' he swiftly denied.

Rank disbelief in her eyes.

He threw out his hands in appeal. 'I swear to you, Angie...'

She recoiled away from him. 'Don't! The contest is over. You won whatever points you wanted to make. Just let me go now, Hugo.'

'No. I don't want to lose you.'

'You have already.'

He sought desperately for words to hold on to her. His mind seized on what she'd said about Paul not loving the person she was. He did. He very much did.

She *was* beautiful, inside and out. In a wildly emotional burst, he offered that truth.

'Angie, I love you.'

She flinched as though he'd hit her. 'Do you say that to all your women?' she flashed at him with acid scepticism.

'I've never said it to any other woman. You're the only one,' he declared with more passion than he'd ever felt before. 'The only one,' he repeated to hammer home how uniquely special she was to him.

He knew Angie had never been with him for the ride he could supply. His wealth truly was irrelevant to her. She was not out to get anything from him except his respect. And the love she deserved. He had to make her see she had both his respect and love.

Before he could find the words to convince her of it she tore her gaze from the blaze of need in his, jerking her head forward. Her throat moved in a convulsive swallow. She spoke with husky conviction. 'This is only about winning. It's all been about winning. A man who loves me would not have put me in that firing line tonight, knowing Paul as you did.'

'Knowing Paul as I did...' God damn the man and the baggage they both carried because of him! '...I hated the thought of you still feeling something for him, Angie. And yes, I wanted to win over him tonight,' he confessed, desperate to set things right. 'I wanted to be certain you're now mine.'

'I'm not a possession,' she flung at him, her cheeks burning scarlet. 'I chose to go with you. Be with you. I told you so before I ever went to bed with you, Hugo.'

But he'd seduced her into his bed. He'd done it very deliberately. Because he'd wanted her. And he'd used sex to tie her to him ever since. But sex wasn't going to work tonight. She'd hate him, despise him, if he tried it.

He told himself to calm down, reason through the important points he needed to make. He was fighting for his life here—*his life with Angie*—and suddenly he knew that was what he wanted more than anything else, and if he didn't make it happen, he'd face a terrible emptiness in all the years to come.

'I do love you, Angie,' he repeated quietly. 'I just didn't like how Paul had belittled you over the billboard photo and tonight I wanted to punch him out with how magnificent you truly are. I didn't plan for you to get hurt. I wanted you to feel proud that you were with me. The truth is…you're the woman I want to spend my life with, not a trophy for show. If you'll do me the honour of marrying me…'

'Don't!' Tears welled into her eyes, and once again she jerked her head away.

'I mean it, Angie,' he pressed, harnessing every bit of persuasive power he had to bring into play.

She shook her head. 'This is still…about winning,' she choked out.

'Yes, it is. Winning you as my wife.'

'It's the wrong time. The wrong time,' she repeated in a kind of frenzied denial.

'Then I'll wait for the right time.'

She looked at him with eyes swimming in pain. 'How can I believe you? Paul threw this challenge at you, Hugo. Paul…' She bit her lips and looked away again.

'Do you imagine I'd let him dictate how I spend the rest of my life, Angie?'

Her fingers plucked at the skirt of her dress, agitatedly folding the fabric. 'This is too much for me. Too much…' Her whole body suddenly jerked forward in alarm. 'James, this is my street,' she cried. 'You've just driven past my apartment block. Stop!'

'Missed the parking spot. Thought I'd just drive around the block, Miss Blessing,' James hastily explained.

'Please…back up!' she begged.

'Sir?'

'Stop and back up, James.'

While he appreciated James' ploy to give him more time, Hugo knew force would only alienate Angie further. Besides, she was right. It *was* the wrong time to make anything stick. He could only hope he'd made strong inroads on the barriers she was still holding on to.

The Bentley was reversed and brought to a halt. James alighted to open the passenger door. Angie rushed out an anxious little speech. 'I don't want you to accompany me to my door, Hugo. I need to be alone now.'

He nodded, not wanting her to be afraid of him, but his eyes locked onto hers with all the searing intensity of his need to convince her of his sincerity. 'Please think about what I've said, Angie. Think about us and how good it's been. And how much more we could have together. Promise me you'll do that.'

The passenger door was opened.

She didn't promise.

She bolted.

'James, see Miss Blessing safely to her door,' he quickly commanded.

'Yes, sir.'

He waited, the need to rein in all his aggressive instincts reducing him to a mass of seething tension. As soon as James had resettled himself in the driver's seat, Hugo asked, 'Did she say anything to you?'

'Miss Blessing thanked me for my many kindnesses, sir.'

'That doesn't sound good.'

'No, sir. Sounded like goodbye to me.'

'I have to win her back, James.'

'Yes, sir. Shall I drive you home now, sir?'

'Might as well. Breaking down her apartment door won't do it.'

'No, sir.'

The Bentley purred into moving on.

Hugo concentrated on coming up with a positive plan of action. 'Flowers tomorrow. Red roses for love. Masses of red roses delivered to her office, James.'

Throat clearing from the driver's seat. 'If I may be so bold, sir, I don't think flowers will do the trick this time. Not even red roses.'

'It's a start,' Hugo argued.

'Yes, sir. Shouldn't hurt,' came the heavily considered reply.

'But it's not enough to swing a change of opinion. I know that, James. You don't need to tell me.'

'No, sir.'

'I have to back them up with something else. Something big. Utterly convincing.' A sense of urgency gripped him. Failure to break this impasse with Angie in double quick time could mean losing her.

'Are you asking me for a suggestion, sir?' came the somewhat dubious question from the front seat.

'If you've got one, James, give it to me,' Hugo bit out.

More throat clearing. 'Please forgive me for…uh…overhearing what was…uh…most certainly a private conversation…'

'Oh, get on with it, James,' Hugo broke in impatiently. 'This is no time for sensibility or sensitivity. I have a crisis on my hands.'

'Right, sir. Well, it seemed to me, Miss Blessing felt you'd made a public show of her for…umh…self-serving reasons, and you'll need to somehow counterbalance that.'

'A show. A public show.'

Hugo seized on the thought, an idea blooming in his mind so fast, it zapped into the mental zone of *perfect move*. There'd been times in his life where he knew intuitively that all the pieces pointed to taking one single winning action—an exhilarating recognition of *rightness*. And when he'd followed through, it had worked for him. Worked brilliantly.

'I've got it, James!' he declared.

'You have, sir?'

'And I'll see to this myself. Push it through. Bribe, coerce…whatever it takes.'

'If I can be of any assistance, sir…'

'What I'm going to do is…'

And he outlined the plan.

Once again, James felt proud and privileged to be in the employ of Hugo Fullbright. Not only did he have the perspicacity to see Miss Blessing as the perfect wife for him, his plan to win her hand in marriage had that marvellous touch of flamboyance that made him such a pleasure to work for.

It was to be hoped—very sincerely hoped—that it would produce the right result.

CHAPTER SEVENTEEN

ANGIE barely slept. The mental and emotional turmoil revolving around everything that had happened with Hugo and Paul gave her no peace. It was impossible to sort out what she should do—give Hugo another chance or end a relationship that felt hopelessly entangled with motives which made her shudder with wretched misery.

She dragged herself out of bed the next morning, red-eyed from bouts of weeping and so fatigued that the idea of facing a day at the office with a happy Francine, fresh from a night of loving with Tim, made her heart quail. But it had to be done. Best that she did occupy herself with work. She'd probably go mad if she fretted any more over whether Hugo truly loved her or not.

The marriage proposal after what Paul had said...it had felt so wrong, so terribly, terribly wrong...how could she believe anything that came out of Hugo's mouth now?

She pushed the whole mess to the back of her mind and determinedly kept it there, even when Francine sailed into the office one hour late and poured out all her excitement and pleasure in Tim's proposal once again, raving about how *perfect* he was for her, how well he understood her, how sweet and generous he was, etc etc etc.

Angie agreed with her, managing as many smiles as she could, feeling sick about not having understood anything about Hugo, except his drive to win. Fortunately, she had a meeting with a contractor after lunch, giving her a break from Francine's blissful contentment. *Unfortunately,* it was at the Pyrmont apartment complex where she was assailed by memories of her first meeting with Hugo.

He hadn't known about Paul then—impossible to doubt that his desire for her company had been genuine. During the whole Tokyo weekend it had definitely been genuine.

Could he be sincere about loving her? Nothing to do with ensuring he didn't lose before he wanted to? These past three months had been so good, everything feeling *right* between them. Even when he'd taken her to the new ballet performance, he'd enjoyed it with her, finding the dancing quite fascinating. And erotic, he'd told her wickedly. Definitely interested in sharing this pleasure with her.

What if he truly didn't want to lose her at all?

What if the marriage proposal was genuine, too?

But he shouldn't have done it last night!

It still felt hopelessly wrong.

At four o'clock Angie returned to the office and winced at seeing a huge arrangement of red roses sitting on her desk. 'You'll have to move Tim's roses somewhere else, Francine,' she tossed at her friend. 'I need the work space.'

'They're for you!' The announcement came with a delighted grin. 'I think Tim's plunge into a marriage proposal has fired up Hugo. Red roses for love, Angie.'

Her heart fluttered nervously, wanting to believe, fearful of believing. Her agitated mind reasoned it was nothing for Hugo to order up flowers. James had probably done it for him. But *red* roses was definitely a first from him.

'There's a note for you,' Angie brightly informed her.

Angie set her briefcase down beside her desk and settled in her chair, needing to feel calmer before reading the attached note. She opened it gingerly. The note was actually hand-written in Hugo's strong scrawl, not some anonymous printing from a florist.

> *I do love you.*
> *I want us to spend the rest of our lives together.*
> *Please don't turn your back on what we have together, Angie.*
> *I'll contact you tomorrow.*
>
> *Hugo*

Tomorrow… Angie drew a deep breath. She had another day to think about it. Not that she was getting anywhere much with her thinking.

'What does he say?' Francine asked eagerly.

Angie shrugged. 'Just that he'll call me tomorrow.'

'He adores you, Angie. Every time he looks at you, it's like he wants to eat you up.'

'That's sex, Francine, not love,' she said with some asperity.

'Oh, yeah? Well let me tell you, when I told him last night about Paul waylaying us and taking you off, he charged out like a bull to get you back with him. That's not sex. That's love.'

Or reclaiming his possession, Angie thought. Francine was rosy-eyed about everything right now. Nevertheless, Angie was reminded that the sense of intimacy she had known with Hugo had extended far beyond the bedroom. If it hadn't been for the too-extravagant gift of jewellery and the nasty encounter with Paul last night, would she be doubting a declaration of love by Hugo?

Wasn't it her own insecurity about the previous women in his life—all of them *temporary* attachments—that had made her see the gift as so much less than a ring of lifelong commitment?

And after all, their relationship *was* only of three months' standing. Three very intense months. But it was still a far cry from Francine's and Tim's situation, the two of them having known each other all through their childhood and teens. It was quite reasonable that Hugo hadn't seriously considered marriage...until she'd challenged him on it in the car last night.

She'd forced the issue.

He'd risen to it.

Why couldn't she accept that it was right for him?

Was she going to let Paul take from her what she most dearly wanted?

If only she could believe Hugo would have asked her to marry him, anyway.

She stared at the note.

He didn't mention marriage...just living together. But he did say...*for the rest of their lives*. And this note wasn't written in the heat of the moment. Hugo had had all night to think about what he wanted.

Tomorrow, Angie thought. *I'll see what happens tomorrow and take it from there.*

Thursday morning...

Angie felt more refreshed, having gone to bed early and slept like a log. Francine had also crashed out at home, and since neither of them had separate plans for today, they both travelled to work in Francine's car. They were in the usual tight stream of traffic crossing the Sydney Harbour Bridge when Francine remarked, 'Change of billboard today. Let's check out who's on it.'

'You don't need to check out anyone anymore,' Angie dryly reminded her.

'I have sympathy for the hopefuls.'

'Well, keep at least half an eye on the traffic as the billboard comes into view.'

She didn't.

She put her foot on the brake and stopped dead, causing mayhem and much honking of horns behind them. And Angie was too shocked to say a word. She didn't even hear the fracas around them. Her stunned gaze was fastened on the one mind-boggling, heart-squeezing photo of a man covering the entire billboard...

Hugo!

A much larger than life Hugo with a bunch of red roses resting in the crook of one arm, his other hand held palm out, offering a small opened box lined with white satin, and nestling in the middle of it, a blindingly gorgeous ring—an emerald with diamonds all around it.

Text was flashing with a kind of spectacular urgency.

Angie—will you marry me?

'Now that...is some proposal!' Francine muttered breathlessly.

Someone rapped on her window and an angry face yelled. 'Have you got trouble, lady? You're holding everyone up.'

Francine rolled down the window and yelled back, 'Have you got no romance in your soul?'

'What?'

'Look at the billboard!' She pointed. 'That's my friend's fiancé up there. Or he soon will be. Right, Angie?'

'Right,' Angie replied faintly.

'You can't get a more public commitment than that,' Francine told her stunned critic.

No, you can't, Angie thought dazedly, and wasn't the slightest bit aware of the rest of the journey to their Glebe office.

Where the red Bentley stood parked at the kerb.

'Stop!' she cried to Francine, totally unprepared for facing Hugo here and now.

Francine brought her car to a screeching halt, causing more mayhem to the traffic behind them on Glebe Road. 'Better get out, Angie,' she advised. 'Guess you won't be working today.'

'I don't know. I don't know,' Angie babbled nervously.

'Out you go and say yes. That's all you have to do. I have no doubt Hugo will take it from there. He's one hell of a go-getter,' Francine said admiringly. 'And all the best to both of you!'

'Thanks, Francine,' Angie mumbled and made herself move, alighting from the car to a blast of honking horns.

Francine stepped on the accelerator, shot forward, braked again as her car came level with the Bentley, honked her horn to draw the notice of the chauffeur, then carried on to drive around to the parking area in the back lane behind the office building.

Angie's suddenly tremulous legs managed to carry

her from the street to the sidewalk. Her heart was galloping as she saw James alight from the driver's side of the Bentley, resplendent in his chauffeur's uniform. He raised a hand to her in a salute of acknowledgment, rounded the gleaming red car, and opened the passenger door on the sidewalk side. He stood at attention beside it, his usual stately dignity slightly sabotaged by the hint of a smile lurking on his lips.

Angie paused to take a deep calming breath and unscramble the assault of wild thoughts in her mind. Was Hugo in the car? Or had James been ordered to take her somewhere to meet him? In which case, should she go or stay? It was a bit presumptuous of Hugo to send his man to collect her when she hadn't even said *yes*.

'*Please* step in, Miss Blessing,' James urged, a slight frown replacing the slight smile. His dignity even cracked so far as to beckon her forward.

Well, it wasn't fair to upset James, Angie reasoned. Besides, it was absurd to play hard to get at this point, when Hugo had well and truly put himself on the line for her. 'I'm coming,' she announced to James, giving him a grin as assurance that all was well.

He actually grinned back!

Which lightened Angie's heart immeasurably as she hurried to oblige him. James definitely approved of her marrying his boss, which should make for a happy household. She dived into the Bentley and straight into another heart-fluttering situation.

Hugo *was* in the car, sitting on the far side of the back seat. 'I've been waiting for you, Angie,' he purred at her as she flopped down beside him, his bedroom blue eyes sizzling with wicked intent. 'Waiting all my life for you to join me.'

'Oh!' was the only sound that came out of her mouth. Her dizzy mind registered that Hugo had just voiced exactly what she'd wished to hear from him. *Exactly!*

James closed the door, locking her in with the man who was fast proving to be the man of her dreams.

'Will you marry me?' he asked, wasting no time in pressing the critical question.

Angie looked askance at him but her heart was dancing, performing cartwheels. 'I'd have to love you first, Hugo.'

His mouth quirked into a very sensual smile. 'I think I love you enough for both of us. Why not give it a chance?'

She laughed. She couldn't help it. A cocktail of happiness was bubbling through her. 'Well, since I love you to distraction, I might just do that.'

'Then you will marry me.'

'Yes. Yes, I will.'

'I need your left hand.'

She gave it to him.

He immediately produced the ring that had glittered so enticingly on the billboard and slid it onto her third finger. 'Perfect fit!' he declared smugly.

'How did you guess?'

'Angie, there is nothing about your body that I don't know intimately. There's nothing about your heart that I don't know intimately. If you'll just let me fully into your mind...'

'I think if you kissed me...'

He did.

And the magic of knowing Hugo really, truly loved

her, and meant to love her all his life, made it the most special kiss of all, making them both sigh with satisfaction when it ended.

Some heavy throat-clearing from the driver's seat signalled that James was ensconced there, ready to drive off. 'To the airport now, sir?'

'Yes. Straight to the airport.' The furred edge of Hugo's voice was very sexy.

'May I be the first to congratulate both of you on your forthcoming nuptials, sir?' James said somewhat pompously, returning to form now that everything was satisfactorily settled.

'You may. Thank you, James.'

'Thank you, James,' Angie warmly chimed in, then turned quizzically to Hugo, 'Why the airport?'

'It's time for meetings with parents. We'll fly to Port Macquarie for mine to drool over you, then on to Byron Bay for yours to look me over. Or we can do it the other way around if you prefer.'

'All in one day?'

'I thought today and tomorrow with one set of parents and the weekend with the other. Enough time for everyone to get to know each other.'

It was a wonderful idea, but...I can't wear the same clothes for four days, Hugo. Can we go home first...?'

'No time. The flight is scheduled.' He gave her his wolf grin. 'You can give me the pleasure of buying whatever you need. That has to be allowable for my future wife!'

Staking out his territory, Angie thought, and laughed, moving to cuddle up to him, blissfully content for Hugo to indulge any pleasure he liked as long as it was with her. 'My warrior!' she murmured happily.

'At your service,' he said just as happily.

Angie sighed. 'Fighting for me from a billboard in full view of everyone crossing the Sydney Harbour Bridge is a story I'm going to relish telling our children.'

'And grandchildren,' he said with equal relish. 'Worth the price,' he added. 'Worth any price to have you, Angie. I just feel the luckiest man on earth to have found you.'

Amen to that, James thought.

The boss sure had a prize in Angie Blessing. And the pitter-patter of tiny feet was clearly on the drawing board. James felt he could now look forward to a fascinating new phase in his life.

FROM BOARDROOM TO BEDROOM

Harlequin Presents® brings you two
original stories guaranteed to make
your Valentine's Day extra special!

THE BOSS'S MARRIAGE ARRANGEMENT
by *Penny Jordan*

Pretending to be her boss's mistress is one thing—but now
everyone in the office thinks Harriet is Matthew Cole's
fiancée! Harriet has to keep reminding herself it's all just
for convenience, but how far is Matthew prepared to go
with the arrangement—marriage?

HIS DARLING VALENTINE
by *Carole Mortimer*

It's Valentine's Day, but Tazzy Darling doesn't care.
Until a secret admirer starts bombarding her with gifts!
Any woman would be delighted—but not Tazzy. There's
only one man she wants to be sending her love tokens, and
that's her boss, Ross Valentine. And her secret admirer
couldn't possibly be Ross…could it?

The way to a man's heart…is through the bedroom

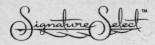

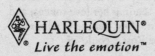

The world's bestselling romance series.

Seduction and Passion Guaranteed!

They're the men who have everything—except a bride....

Wealth, power, charm—what else could a heart-stoppingly
handsome tycoon need? In the GREEK TYCOONS
miniseries you have already been introduced to some
gorgeous Greek multimillionaires who are in need of wives.

THE GREEK BOSS'S DEMAND
by *Trish Morey*
On sale January 2005, #2444

THE GREEK TYCOON'S CONVENIENT MISTRESS
by *Lynne Graham*
On sale February 2005, #2445

THE GREEK'S SEVEN-DAY SEDUCTION
by *Susan Stephens*
On sale March 2005, #2455

Pick up a Harlequin Presents® novel and you will enter a world
of spine-tingling passion and provocative, tantalizing romance!

Available wherever Harlequin books are sold.

www.eHarlequin.com